ALSO BY J.S. SCOTT

ご

The Sinclairs

The Billionaire's Christmas (A Sinclair Novella)
No Ordinary Billionaire
The Forbidden Billionaire
The Billionaire's Touch
The Billionaire's Voice
The Billionaire Takes All
The Billionaire's Secrets
Only a Millionaire

The Billionaire's Obsession

Mine for Tonight
Mine for Now
Mine Forever
Mine Completely
Heart of the Billionaire – Sam
Billionaire Undone – Travis
The Billionaire's Salvation – Max
The Billionaire's Game – Kade
Billionaire Unmasked – Jason
Billionaire Untamed – Tate
Billionaire Unbound – Chloe
Billionaire Undaunted – Zane
Billionaire Unknown – Blake
Billionaire Unveiled – Marcus
Billionaire Unloved – Jett
Billionaire Unchallenged – Carter

The Walker Brothers

Release!
Player
Damaged

The Sentinel Demons

A Dangerous Bargain
A Dangerous Hunger
A Dangerous Fury
A Dangerous Demon King
The Sentinel Demons – The Complete Boxed Set

Big Girls and Bad Boys

The Curve Ball
The Beast Loves Curves
Curves by Design
The Curve Collection Boxed Set

The Pleasure of His Punishment: Individual Stories or Complete Boxed Set

The Changeling Encounters

Mate of the Werewolf
The Danger of Adopting a Werewolf
All I Want for Christmas is a Werewolf
The Changeling Encounters – Complete Boxed Set

The Vampire Coalition

Ensnared

THE

ACCIDENTAL

BILLIONAIRES

BOOK ONE

J.S. SCOTT

 Montlake
Romance

Published by Montlake Romance, Seattle

www.apub.com

Amazon, the Amazon logo, and Montlake Romance are trademarks of Amazon.com, Inc., or its affiliates.

ISBN-13: 9781503905474
ISBN-10: 1503905470

Cover photography and design by Laura Klynstra

Printed in the United States of America

This book is dedicated to my fabulous friend, Judy.
Thanks for being there during the bad times,
and the better ones.
True friends are hard to find, and even though we don't
see each other often, I always know you're there.
I miss you. I think it's time for a vacay.
Love ya!!

XXXXXXX Jan

PROLOGUE

JADE

Five months ago . . .

"Just a few more minutes, Ms. Sinclair," the secretary informed me as she hung up the phone. "Mr. Stone is running somewhat behind today."

Somewhat behind?

I'd been waiting for *close to an hour.* I'd pretty much read every magazine in the waiting room from cover to cover, even the articles I wouldn't normally bother to read. Did women really want to know how to attract a man, or how to get the attention of one of *them* who didn't want to be with *her?*

Pretty weird articles, really. Or was I the one who didn't really understand? Judging by my not-so-exciting dating life, maybe I should have paid more attention to all those women's magazines. I didn't exactly have men beating down my door to go out with me. But then, it had always been that way.

Can I have a dating slump when I never really had an incredible dating life in the first place?

Because of work and school, I hadn't been able to try out a lot of different guys, and to be honest, they hadn't wanted to date me, either. I'd made one major mistake in college. I had to either blame that one on complete exhaustion and stress, or admit to myself that I'd let somebody use me for two years.

I preferred the former excuse.

I don't really want to attract a guy who doesn't notice me the first time he meets me.

Wasn't there supposed to be some kind of spark, some unknown recognition that somebody was my soulmate? And wouldn't they realize it, too?

I certainly hope so, otherwise I'm waiting for something that's never going to happen.

Unfortunately, thanks to the score of women's magazines in the room, I now *knew* how to get a man who *didn't* want me, and what the moon and stars had in mind for my future mate, according to the horoscopes.

Maybe the article about improving my orgasms would have been useful if I had any, but I could have skipped the piece on giving a guy a better blow job.

Not exactly something I'd normally peruse, but I'd had an hour to kill, and after I'd read the interesting stuff like *National Geographic*, I'd still had time on my hands, so I'd pushed my way through the women's magazines, too.

I was pretty sure I *wasn't* better off because I was now armed with the wisdom on how to deal with a commitment-phobic male, and I was getting restless.

I smiled and nodded at the secretary politely from my seat in the plush outer office of billionaire and business mogul Eli Stone. It wasn't the elderly assistant's fault that her boss had left me waiting for way longer than anybody should have to wait for a scheduled appointment, even with a billionaire.

I'm a billionaire, too. Isn't there some kind of unspoken courtesy thing among the megarich? Does one billionaire leave another one waiting for an hour to see them?

Unfortunately, I hadn't been rich long enough to know the rules.

Mr. Stone had a net worth a lot higher than mine, but once somebody reached billionaire status, did it really matter?

I dropped the last magazine I'd finished on the table with a sigh.

I'm completely out of reading material, even the ridiculous stuff.

I tapped my foot impatiently, wondering if this *was* the way billionaires treated each other.

Truth was, I'd only been a billionaire for a matter of months, and I still had no idea what I was supposed to do with my newfound wealth. To be honest, all my money and investments terrified the hell out of me. I was a science-and-wildlife geek. Ask me any question about conservation or animal behavior, and I could go on for hours. But I had no idea what to do with a fortune.

I only knew how to live poor, so I was basically paralyzed with fear every time I glanced at my bank account and my investment portfolio. I knew I *should* be happy, but for some unknown reason, I wasn't.

Through an accident of birth, and because of the father I'd never known, I'd suddenly become one of the richest women in the world. I was now a wealthy and powerful Sinclair.

Well, I'd *always* been a Sinclair, but the wealthy part of it—not so much. Never in a million years would I have guessed that I was related to the super-rich Sinclairs on the East Coast.

Me, my twin sister, Brooke, and my brothers, Noah, Seth, Aiden, and Owen, had gone from being dirt poor our entire lives to having more money than God because we'd discovered that our father had been a bigamist. My father was a man who had acquired two wives and two separate families on opposite coasts.

My siblings and I had kind of gotten the bad part of *that* deal. Well, financially, anyway.

It's not that I wasn't grateful that the East Coast Sinclairs had found our family on the West Coast. My half brother Evan had brought us all together as one very large family. But our inheritance, which had made me and all of my siblings ridiculously wealthy, was still something I just wasn't used to.

I'd invested the majority of my legacy with Evan's help, and he still assisted me by managing my overwhelming portfolio, even though all of my half brothers and my half sister were on the East Coast. He'd set up my money to make *more money*, and I sometimes got dizzy watching it grow. And that was pretty much *all I did*. I watched my fortune increase every single day. I felt too intimidated by all those zeros to do anything else.

Unlike my brothers, I didn't much care if the money continued to multiply, and I didn't have big plans like they did.

I wish I did. Maybe it would be easier if I was constantly busy and planning out my future.

The only major purchase I'd made was a waterfront cottage in my hometown of Citrus Beach. Again, Evan had made that happen. I'd picked out a home I'd love to have, like my half brother had requested, and he'd pushed the sale through at a pace I found mind boggling. Really, it was a lovely house I'd much rather have been enjoying right now instead of waiting on Eli Stone in the middle of downtown San Diego.

Glancing at my watch for about the millionth time, I hoped Mr. Stone would give me what I wanted, and I could make it home in time to watch the sunset. But if it took much longer, I was going to get stuck in San Diego traffic, and I wouldn't see my house until it was already dark.

"He's ready for you, Ms. Sinclair." The secretary stood up as she spoke.

I rose and grabbed my purse. I was probably underdressed to be inside the Stone corporate headquarters, but at least I'd been comfortable waiting in my well-worn jeans, sandals, and a baby-blue top.

I nodded at the woman, who opened the enormous double doors and then closed them behind me like a gatekeeper.

I moved forward and perched on the edge of one of the massive chairs in front of Eli Stone's desk before I finally looked up at the man I'd waited an hour to see. I gaped at the guy I'd only seen on television or on the cover of a magazine in the supermarket.

He cleans up good.

Most of the time, Eli Stone had only gotten my attention because of the outrageous hobbies and challenges he pursued. If there was an element of danger to an activity, this man always seemed to be up for trying it.

Race-car driving.

Big-wave surfing.

Skydiving.

Extreme water-sport challenges.

Hang gliding.

Rocketry.

For God's sake, the guy had purchased his own rocket company and was planning on sending unmanned flights out into the Milky Way shortly. From what I'd heard, Eli Stone was way ahead in the private space game, so he obviously took that pursuit seriously.

"Mr. Stone," I said in a modulated tone. "Thank you for seeing me."

I was pretty sure I'd never seen him in a suit, since he seemed to enjoy flashing his half-naked body in his photos and videos. Personally, I found the gray suit and elegant gray-and-navy tie much more appealing.

Not that he didn't look good half-naked, too. But it was pretty hard to take somebody doing an insane stunt all that seriously.

But *this* Eli Stone, the one sitting in front of me, had my complete attention.

He looked aloof, but he was watching me like an eagle eyes potential prey from the air right before it finally strikes. And I really didn't like being the rabbit that he'd just spied from above.

Starting at the top of my head, he assessed me slowly. "Ms. Sinclair," he acknowledged in a smooth baritone. "What can I do for you?"

Many things came to mind as I stared back at him, but I answered, "I sent you a proposal on the property I'd like to buy. Have you had a chance to look at it?"

I really *had* to stop staring into his cool gray eyes, thinking about how well his suit matched his eye color.

I didn't know why, but I was completely fascinated by *this* Eli Stone. Unlike his television persona, this man was all too real.

He made me nervous for reasons I couldn't explain. There was tension in the air between us, even though we had never met. And I wasn't at all comfortable with the heat that was pooling between my thighs.

I'd never been struck with instant lust. But there was something about Eli Stone that completely captivated me.

Maybe because the guy in front of me isn't at all what I expected.

He was a clown on television, and he was always smirking arrogantly in his photos. I'd expected to meet a person who took almost nothing seriously. Instead, I'd gotten a man who commanded attention just by being present in the room. And he looked like he had absolutely nothing to smile about.

I could practically smell his earthy scent, although I knew it wasn't really traveling from his body to my nose all the way across the big desk.

I watched as he casually opened his jacket and leaned back in his chair. I swallowed hard as I waited for his reply, but he didn't seem in any hurry to give me one.

I knew that he had a droolworthy body. Generally, I wasn't big on tattoos, but the tribal markings that I'd seen on his arm had always looked good on him.

Funny, but I'd never been hit with the primal urge to screw him when I'd seen his ripped body in magazines or on TV. But being up close and personal was . . . different.

"I didn't read it," he said sharply. "I'm not interested in letting go of that piece of property. It's been in my family for decades. It's not developable right now, although it could be in the future. My question to you is—why do *you* want it?"

Shit! Since the land near Lucifer's Canyon was pretty much useless, I'd been hoping to easily convince him to part with it. Compared to the businesses, vast properties, and the land he owned, that acreage in the backcountry was less than nothing.

"I'm a wildlife genetic conservationist," I explained. "A portion of the land is an important wildlife corridor. I'd like to make sure it's always preserved."

Who knew what Eli Stone would do with the land in the future? For all I knew, he'd turn it into a launching pad for his spaceflights. It was important to me to see that the passage leading from one open space to another was kept intact.

"Ah, yes," he said in a condescending tone. "The wildlife conservationist and primitive survivalist who suddenly became a Sinclair, right? I had my people check you out before I accepted your appointment. You have an interesting history."

"I've *always* been a Sinclair," I said through gritted teeth.

Jerk! Why in the world did he need my life story just to tell me he doesn't want to sell some property? It has to have been the most boring report he's ever read.

Maybe I hadn't *always* been part of the high-profile Sinclairs, but my siblings and I had faced a lot of challenges, and we'd always gotten through it. I was pretty proud of that.

"Just not one of the *wealthy ones* until recently," he pointed out. "The Sinclairs on the East Coast have been a powerful family for generations. How did you say you became part of that family?"

"I didn't," I snapped. It was none of Eli Stone's business how I was related to the Sinclair dynasty. And my father's bigamist behavior wasn't something I wanted to talk about, especially not with *him*.

The West Coast and East Coast Sinclairs shared the same father. That's all anybody really knew. My brothers here in California had made it a point not to turn the tragic story into a tabloid scandal. My twin sister, Brooke, had been on the East Coast recovering from her own trauma, and none of us wanted her to find out from the gossip papers that she was going to inherit a fortune. She needed time to heal from losing her friends and coworkers in a bank robbery where she'd nearly lost her own life as well. Brooke didn't even know about the money yet. My siblings and I had all agreed to give her time to deal with the tragedy before throwing anything else on her.

Honestly, I was surprised that Eli had been able to dig up *any* information about me or my family. My half brother Evan had gone to a lot of trouble to make sure nobody got to the truth until Brooke was emotionally healed and back on the West Coast again.

Evan had obviously been successful, since Eli Stone apparently hadn't been able to get access to all the details.

"I might be willing to bargain on other properties, but not that one," he said thoughtfully.

I folded my arms in front of me. "Since that's the *only one* I'm interested in, then I guess we're done here."

Maybe I *was* disappointed that I couldn't secure the wildlife corridor, but I had the sudden need to get out from under the intensity of his gaze. I was pissed off about him digging into my personal life, but I was squirming from his blatant stare. I quickly came to the conclusion that my need to escape was currently more important than my outrage.

Before I could get up, he said casually, "You're really quite beautiful, Jade."

That stunned me into silence, and I gaped at him as my palms began to sweat. "I don't understand."

His expression had changed mercurially, and so fast it was almost scary.

He smiled, a calculated grin that I was pretty sure he always used to his advantage. I was certain almost any woman would drop her panties the moment she saw his attractive smile.

Fortunately, I'm not almost any woman.

"It's quite simple, actually. I find you attractive," he answered.

Nobody had ever said that to me during my twenty-six years on the planet. My twin, Brooke, was the pretty one. I was the *other twin*, the one who went out in the wilderness and practiced making traps, finding drinkable water, and kept adding to my survival skills.

It was something I usually did *alone*.

Especially after getting dumped by my one and only boyfriend in college.

I wasn't the kind of woman that a guy did a double take on when I walked down the street, and I was sort of okay with that. I liked being me, even if I wasn't the kind of woman who attracted much attention with my physical appearance.

Not that I went out of my way to get noticed. I was quiet and shy by nature unless I was with friends or family. Most of the time, I preferred the company of animals instead of humans.

Yeah, I had the hope that there was a soulmate out there somewhere for me, somebody who would see *me* underneath my timid, tomboy exterior. But I wasn't holding my breath until I met him.

"Can we get back to the subject of the property?" I asked, trying not to let his appreciative looks intimidate me. "If that was a firm *no* answer, then I won't waste any more of your time."

He moved forward and linked his fingers together on the desk, his intent gray eyes never straying from my face. "I make you nervous," he observed.

"Maybe I'm not used to meeting billionaires," I said.

He shook his dark head. "It's not that. I don't think you're impressed by my money. I found it intriguing that you inherited your own fortune but the only thing you've purchased was a home. In Citrus Beach. A sound investment, since the area is growing fast."

Okay. I had to admit that it was a little creepy that he knew so much about me.

"It wasn't an *investment,*" I argued. "It was a *home.* My home. And I hope Citrus Beach never gets too big. I like it the way it is."

I found it unnerving that he seemed to know every move that I'd made since coming into money, and that he'd had the audacity to have me investigated. Who does that just to meet with somebody about a property proposal?

My outrage was starting to take over my desire to get up and run out of Eli Stone's office.

He shrugged. "Time marches forward, Ms. Sinclair. It's what makes us richer. Citrus Beach will eventually grow. It's close enough to San Diego to make it a desirable place to live."

"I don't *need* to get richer. I'm already so rich it makes me a little nauseous. I just want that piece of land."

"The money makes you uncomfortable?" he asked.

"No," I lied. The last thing I needed him to focus on was how uncomfortable I was with my wealth.

"You recently finished a fellowship," he said, completely ignoring my statement. "Your education is pretty impressive. But what do you do with a degree in wildlife?"

Scratch the idea that he'd only checked out what I'd done since I'd inherited. He knew my whole damn life!

"I have a *doctorate* in wildlife conservation," I corrected. "My focus is genetics. I think we can someday use genetic material to save species that can't recover their numbers with the usual methods."

He nodded. "Admirable. And the survivalist training?"

Was there anything that he *didn't* know?

"It's a hobby. I teach classes now because it's something I love."
I had no idea why I felt I needed to confirm my life story with an

unsettling billionaire, but the words just kept popping out of my mouth.

"I respect that."

"I'm not looking for *anybody's* esteem," I informed him icily. "I just came to buy a piece of land. But since you've already refused to sell, we *are* done." I stood, unable to sit still with him watching me.

He got up and moved around his desk as he said, "You're defensive. Did I make you uncomfortable, Dr. Sinclair?"

Rarely did anyone use my doctorate title, so I hesitated, trying to decide if he was mocking me, or if he was doing it out of respect for my education.

I finally told myself it didn't matter, and I moved toward the exit. I really needed to get the hell away from Eli Stone.

His large, powerful body stopped in front of me, blocking my path to the door, which ignited my temper. And I almost never got pissed off. But I was tired of playing whatever game he seemed to be enjoying.

I had no idea how to win this match, and I didn't plan on being around long enough to complete it.

"As a matter of fact, yes—you did make me uncomfortable," I replied. "I don't appreciate anyone investigating my private life over a proposal. It was completely inappropriate and more than a little creepy."

"You're right," he conceded. "But I was curious."

"Not a good reason to invade my privacy," I informed him coolly.

"Maybe it wasn't," he agreed, not sounding the least bit contrite.

Everything about this man made me squirm, and I wasn't generally a nervous female. But Eli Stone was the most intense guy I'd ever met.

"Are you upset because I was open about the fact that I wouldn't mind having you in my bed?"

His bluntness made my heartbeat kick faster.

Dear Lord, I'm out of my league.

I tried to keep my expression blank. I didn't want him to have the satisfaction of knowing he could rattle me.

"Did it ever occur to *you* that I might not want you in *mine*?" I asked him indignantly. "Does every woman you know fall at your feet after you tell them that they're attractive? Because it's really not all that unique."

"Did you know that your eyes get a deeper shade of blue when you're angry?" he asked with a grin.

Dammit!

Eli Stone was playing with me, but for what purpose I didn't know.

"Have a good day, Mr. Stone. Personally, I wish I hadn't wasted so much of mine waiting for you when you were already certain you weren't going to sell," I said as I pushed around him and made my way to the door.

He caught my arm as I reached for the door handle. "I was curious as to why you wanted that property," he explained. "Wealthy people generally don't seek property that has very little chance of making them money someday."

"It's *not* useless. Not to me," I argued. "In fact, it's pretty damn important for the purpose of preserving wildlife."

He shrugged. "I don't know anybody who cares about that."

"Then maybe you need to get some new friends," I retorted.

I shook off his hold, and then turned back to him, angry that he valued nobody's time but his own. "You could have called me and asked why I wanted it. I didn't need to come to the city and then wait for an hour just to hear you tell me *no*. It's rude. It's inconsiderate. And it's incredibly arrogant."

"I guess you still need to learn that people wait for billionaires," he stated flatly.

I put a finger to my chest. "Not *this* billionaire. I guess I'm just not as self-serving or conceited as you are. But I don't like people waiting for me. It makes me feel guilty."

I didn't mention that I was pretty motivated by guilt all the time.

I was pretty sure that Eli Stone never suffered much from remorse, so he probably had no idea what I was talking about anyway.

"Have dinner with me, Jade," he said, his statement a command and not a request.

"I have plans," I threw back in his face. "And I'm hungry. I'm not willing to wait like a pathetic puppy until you decide to feed me."

He crossed his arms in front of him with a smile, his eyes dancing with amusement. "Now that I know what a nasty temper you have, I wouldn't dare make you wait," he said drily. "I promise that I'll feed you immediately."

"I came here to make a business deal, not to spend a night in a playboy billionaire's bed."

"I'm not playing, Jade," he said in a low, dangerous tone.

"Not interested," I said angrily as I opened the door. "And you really need to get a lot more interesting reading material in your office if making people cool their heels in your waiting room is a chronic thing for you. I'm pretty sure I lost a few points off my IQ from reading your fluffy women's magazines."

I didn't look back as I rushed through the door, almost certain I could hear a very male laugh as I left Eli Stone's office like my ass was on fire.

CHAPTER 1

JADE

The present . . .

"I'm not interested," I said flatly into my cell phone just before I hit the "Off" button so hard I winced at the strain to my finger.

I glared at the electronic device as I tossed it on the kitchen counter. Right now, my phone was the enemy, and I wished I hadn't dashed off my couch to answer it. But since it was the middle of the afternoon on a workday, I'd been hoping it was a request for a job interview. I had applications and résumés out everywhere. But I hadn't exactly been bombarded by opportunities where I could really use my education.

I'm in a highly specialized field, and getting funding for new studies is difficult.

Eventually, I'd get the right opportunity. Until then, I'd be jumping every time my phone rang. Unfortunately, it was never a person I wanted to talk to right now. But if I didn't recognize the number, I had to pick up.

The call I'd just cut off had been *another* local guy, somebody who claimed to know me from high school, who wanted to know if I would go out with him.

It was the third such call I'd had since yesterday.

And what felt like the millionth I'd received in the last several weeks.

I sighed. Yes, I'd wanted a more active dating life. But not like this. Word had gotten out that I was suddenly a very rich woman, and not one single guy who had called had been interested before I'd come into money.

Now, every unmarried male wanted to date me.

Okay, maybe not date *me*. They wanted to court *my money*.

Honestly, I was starting to hate being rich.

Before I could start dwelling on the fact that no guy actually wanted me for me, I strode back to the living room and flopped down on the couch.

"Job interview?" my brother Aiden asked from his seat in the recliner.

"It was nobody," I answered. "Just another guy who wants to date my money."

I looked at the TV. "What are you watching?"

"The new big-wave competition in Northern California that Eli Stone hosted. They caught some big-ass waves that were well over fifty feet. It was pretty crazy. Stone is up right now," he replied.

I looked at the television, a big screen that my brothers had insisted I get, even though it barely fit on the wall of my small cottage.

"That's the outer edge of the Channel Islands," I said as I frowned at the TV. "He's insane."

"Not much room for error," Aiden agreed. "If he doesn't catch the wave, he'll end up between a gigantic wall of water and the rocks."

My heart was in my throat as I watched Eli paddling into the enormous incoming wave.

My brothers all surfed, and they'd tried to teach me and Brooke, but neither one of us had been nearly as enthusiastic as our male siblings.

"Well, fuck me," Aiden exclaimed. "He made it."

I let out a breath I hadn't even realized I'd been holding as Eli rode the massive wave. "He's going to kill himself," I said anxiously.

"News flash," Aiden said drily. "This happened last winter. He lived. These are just highlights."

I made a face at my brother before I turned back to the television again to watch the interview that was happening with Eli Stone.

And there it was.

It was the Eli Stone persona that I was used to seeing. He'd already pulled his arms out of his wet suit, and it was bunched around his waist. His chiseled upper body was hard not to notice, and my eyes roamed over the signature tattoo down his arm.

But the thing that really stood out was the arrogant smirk on his face. And the lack of emotion in his gorgeous gray eyes.

There was nothing that told me he was flying high from his latest extreme-sports victory. The cocky smile was there, but it didn't go all the way to his eyes.

My brother switched the TV off. "Let's hit the pool."

Aiden had dropped over to go for a swim. It wasn't like he didn't have his own pool, but I had a feeling he wanted to check on me.

None of my brothers liked the weird guys I was attracting because of the money I'd inherited. But I wasn't sure what they planned to do about it. I'd changed my number twice, and it wasn't like anybody was going to kidnap me. They'd need me alive if they wanted my money.

It was more of an irritant than fear-inducing.

I hadn't really had any privacy for the last few months. Somehow, word had leaked to the public about my family's inheritance, and if I wasn't fielding men who seemed to be coming out of the woodwork, I was refusing requests from reporters for an interview about how we'd become connected with the rich, powerful Sinclair family on the East Coast.

Aiden and I didn't talk much as we settled by the pool and did our laps side by side.

I stopped before my brother did, and took a rest.

When he came to a halt, he finally asked, "So who are you dating?"

For some reason, all my brothers thought they were entitled to know every detail of my personal life even though they never shared theirs.

"Nobody," I said grumpily. "They all just want my money."

"Obviously all of them don't. What's up with Eli Stone?" he questioned as he hefted his muscular body out of my swimming pool and went to dry himself off.

"What do you mean?" I asked as I floated on a small raft in the middle of the pool. The water was heated, and I wasn't quite ready to get out yet.

"Come on, Jade," Aiden said. "You had the speaker on when you listened to his message earlier. Are you dating him? The guy makes us look like paupers. You can't say *he's* after your inheritance."

No, he's after my body.

Really, Eli's motives weren't nearly as repulsive to me anymore. At least he'd been bluntly honest. Unlike other men who had started asking me out only because of my money. However, that didn't make me any more likely to answer Eli's phone calls or messages. He made me uncomfortable in ways that I still didn't quite understand.

Honestly, I'd been surprised to hear Eli's voice on my messages earlier. For the last several months, he'd been persistent, and he was *still* calling, even though I'd never answered a single one of his messages over the last five months. But since I hadn't heard from him for almost a month now, I was pretty sure he'd given up.

Apparently, I was wrong.

And the current message from him had been the same as all the others.

He *still* wanted me to have dinner with him.

And I *still* wanted to avoid him, so I hadn't ever called him back.

I would have thought he'd gotten the unspoken message by now. What guy keeps trying when a woman is ignoring him?

I'd seen Eli once a few months ago. He'd been having dinner with a friend in one of his restaurants in San Diego, and I'd been with all of my family celebrating my sister Brooke's engagement to a man she'd met while she'd been on the East Coast.

My twin was now married to Liam Sullivan, and she'd chosen to stay in Maine with her new husband.

Eli and I *had* actually eaten in the same restaurant, just like he'd wanted. We just hadn't been sitting at the same table.

The accidental meeting had unsettled me, especially when I'd felt him watching me during our family get-together. We hadn't spoken, but Eli had made it clear that he knew I was there before he'd departed.

Maybe I hadn't answered any of his messages. But I'd thought about him a lot. I wasn't sure why, since all he wanted was to get me into his bed, and I didn't do one-night stands. But the way my body had reacted to him was . . . unusual.

"I'm not *dating* him," I confessed to my older brother. "I met him once, and he's called me several times to ask if I'd do dinner with him. I haven't even answered his messages."

"Ouch! That's cold," Aiden answered.

If I told my older brother that Eli just wanted to screw me, which I wouldn't because there was no way I was going to discuss sex with my brother, he wouldn't have said I was cold. He would have wanted to beat the hell out of Eli Stone.

"I'm just not interested," I told him as I slid off the raft and climbed out of the pool. "He makes me uncomfortable."

Aiden flopped on a chaise lounge as he queried, "Is he stalking you? If he is, you know Seth and I can take care of him."

I rolled my eyes as I finished toweling off my wet body, and then dropped into the lounger beside him. "No guy is going to stalk me."

Aiden chuckled. "Most likely because you can bust all of their balls."

My brother was right. I wasn't exactly the helpless type, and I didn't *need* a man. In fact, the majority of guys I'd met *did* give me a wide berth most of the time. Most of the men I'd met in the past were survivalists, just like me, and even though they might admire my skills, none of them really saw me as a female. They saw me as competition.

"Do you think that's why nobody really wants to go out with me? Because I don't *need* them?" I questioned.

I'd been on a dating hiatus since I'd broken up with the jerk I'd dated in college. The break wasn't really by choice. I just hadn't met anybody who showed very much interest in me as a potential date. And I certainly hadn't met anybody intriguing, unless I wanted to count Eli Stone, which I didn't.

"Honestly, yes," Aiden said bluntly. "Some men want to feel like they can contribute something to a relationship with their superior skills. But you don't want to date somebody like that. If they're intimidated, they're fucking insecure. You need somebody who doesn't need to have their ego stroked constantly, not a primitive survivalist who gets annoyed because you know more than they do about hunting, trapping, foraging, and other survival stuff. You need somebody who admires your strengths instead of being intimidated by them."

I shuddered as I remembered Eli saying he *admired* me. He might be an arrogant prick, but he hadn't seemed the least bit daunted.

"I'm not very attractive, because I hate fussing with clothes and makeup," I mused. "Brooke was always way better with people than me. I was the geek who wanted to get out into the woods and explore."

"There's plenty of things to like about you," Aiden grumbled. "And I'm not just saying that because you're my sister. But some men are put off by women who are perfectly capable of taking care of themselves."

"So I have to act helpless?" I asked, horrified at the thought.

The idea of being some kind of shrinking violet was never going to feel good or right to me.

"Hell, no," Aiden answered as he reached for his water bottle and took a long slug. "You don't need to be anyone except yourself. So tell me about Stone. Why are you afraid of him?"

I grabbed my diet soda and drank some before I answered, "I'm not *afraid* of him. I just think he's a jerk. I was trying to acquire a piece of property out near Lucifer's Canyon, so I could make sure one of the wildlife corridors stays intact. I sent an offer and made an appointment. But he wasn't willing to sell."

"So you're mad because he didn't want to sell you some acreage?"

"No. I was pissed because he made me drive all the way to his offices, wait an hour until he'd see me, and then turned my offer down flat. He could have had somebody call me and let me know he didn't want to sell. But he was curious about why I wanted to buy it. The jackass took up a ton of my time because he wanted to ask a question. Who does that?"

"Damn billionaires think they run the world," he said with a grin as he put on his sunglasses.

I couldn't help but smile back at him. My family handled our sudden wealth with as much humor as possible. It's the only thing we'd ever had to lighten our decidedly heavy burdens when we were younger.

"I don't think I could ever do that to somebody, money or not," I told him.

"Do you want me to have a talk with him?" he asked. "If you're sure you don't want to speak to him, I can get him to leave you alone."

I was raised by my three older brothers, so I was accustomed to hearing all of them trying to protect me in some way or another.

"No," I answered, my voice sounding somewhat panicked. The last thing I wanted was one of my brothers threatening somebody like Eli

Stone. We might all have money now, but Eli had a lot more friends in high places. "He'll give up eventually. And I can handle myself."

"Are you sure that's what you want?"

"Of course. That's why I haven't answered him."

"He's persistent," Aiden observed. "And you must have made one hell of an impression if he's still calling months after you met."

"I don't think I did," I explained. "Honestly, I don't understand what he wants. I think it's some kind of game for him."

"His message sounded pretty sincere. He didn't sound like a stalker."

I had to admit that my brother was correct. Every time Eli left a message, he sounded as cool as a cucumber, and businesslike, almost like he wanted to schedule a meeting. If I didn't recall every word he'd said to me the day we met, I'd have a very hard time believing he even saw me as a female.

"Aiden, he could have almost any woman he wants. Why would he want me? Why would he even want to play a cat-and-mouse game? Do you think he's twisted?"

"Did it ever occur to you that he might just like you?"

"No," I admitted. "He's Eli Stone."

"He sounded like a guy who was asking you out to dinner. And no man is too good for my sister. Not ever. You're beautiful, intelligent, driven, and empathetic. What in the hell else could any guy want? You can't blame the man for his persistence. I kind of like the fact that he knows that you're worth the work."

I sighed as I leaned my head back against the lounger. My brothers always gave me an ego boost. In their eyes, Brooke and I would always be perfect. "Maybe he makes me uncomfortable because he actually seemed to find me attractive."

Brooke and I had always been careful about sharing too much with any of our brothers, because they had a tendency to insert themselves into any situation they judged as bad for their two sisters. But my relationship with Aiden had changed somewhat since Brooke had left

California for good. I wasn't sure if Aiden was realizing that we were all grown up now, or he was just mellowing out as he got older.

We'd become a lot closer, and we talked about a lot of things I'd previously only shared with Brooke. Granted, there was no way I was discussing my sex life—or lack of it—with any of my brothers, but we did talk more about personal stuff.

Not that he or any of my brothers didn't think they always knew what was best for their little twin sisters, even though I'd already graduated with a doctorate, finished a fellowship, and was now on the job hunt for a position as a scientist. And Brooke was married and living across the country.

I was pretty sure that some of their high-handedness would probably *never* change, no matter what Brooke and I did.

But Aiden, Seth, and I *had* become much tighter since I didn't see Brooke very often now.

"You *are* attractive," Aiden said sternly. "And Brooke was *not* the pretty twin. I've heard you say that way too many times, and you need to get that thought out of your head. You two are twins, and even though you're not identical, you look pretty similar. Your personalities are just different."

I couldn't argue with my brother's point. Brooke and I had always been incredibly close even though our interests were dissimilar. And we'd gone in different directions after high school because we *were* different.

Brooke had gotten a degree in finance and had come back to Citrus Beach to work at one of the local banks.

I'd gone on to do a fellowship when she was already finished with her degree in finance, determined to do what I could to preserve animal species that were endangered.

My brothers had always claimed I was gifted. But I didn't see it that way. College had just come easy for me, and science even more so. I'd finished my master's degree by the time I was twenty-two, and my doctorate at twenty-four. My last two years had been spent doing a postdoc fellowship. I'd essentially spent my entire adult life studying and getting educated.

I'd always known I wasn't going to get rich as a conservationist. I'd spent a lot of volunteer hours at various conservation organizations, doing everything from analyzing animal fecal matter to hand-feeding babies.

My twin had never shared my interest in ecology and wildlife, and we'd often gone our separate ways after high school.

But nothing had ever broken the twin bond we had, and I was sure that nothing ever would, even though we were physically separated now.

It was weird that I never really felt the distance when we'd gone to separate colleges, but it seemed profound now that I knew she was never going to come home again.

I was happy that Brooke had found her soulmate, but I missed her, and her absence now seemed so . . . final. I guess I'd never considered the fact that she might end up living somewhere other than Citrus Beach.

My twin had found the love of her life in Amesport, Maine.

And I was still in Citrus Beach and completely jobless and dateless.

Maybe that was why I felt so left behind.

I had way too much time on my hands right now.

Granted, after I'd gotten burned by a deadbeat in college, I'd been wary of almost any guy who had paid attention to me. Not that it happened often, except for the ones who just wanted to marry money.

I wasn't *really* alone. I had three older brothers who lived close to me now, and a younger brother who had finished medical school and was currently in his residency out of state, but it wasn't quite the same as having Brooke here with me.

I guess I'd always assumed that my twin and I would eventually be living in the same place once our education was done. It had been far more likely that I'd have to accept a job out of state or even out of the country.

It had never occurred to me that Brooke would be the one to move away.

"Maybe you should give Stone a chance," Aiden said.

"He's too . . . intense. Plus, you know about all of the crazy things he does. He's pretty high-profile for his ridiculous stunts."

Aiden shrugged. "He has a lot of hobbies. Hell, he's been rich since the day he was born, so maybe he gets bored."

"He runs a huge international conglomerate," I reminded my brother. "How in the world could he get *bored*?"

"It's not a crime to have fun, Jade," Aiden said in a serious tone. "Maybe none of us are used to having downtime, but most people do. I know we all had to bust our asses when we were younger, and times were tough. But it doesn't have to be that way anymore, baby girl."

I ignored the nickname my older brothers had always used for Brooke and me. Honestly, they had been referring to us by that name for so long, I'd probably miss it if they didn't use it.

"I feel guilty because I'm not off working somewhere right now," I told him. "It's weird knowing that no matter what I do, I'll still be rich unless I do something completely idiotic. I'm not used to it. Are you?"

"Nope. I'll probably *never* get used to it. But I'm not complaining. I didn't really want to be a commercial fisherman all my life. And now I don't have to be. I like being my own boss a lot better, even though I have to put up with Seth's ugly mug every damn day."

"He says the same thing," I informed him.

"He sucks," Aiden said gruffly.

Neither one of my brothers *had* to work together. But I honestly don't think they'd know what to do without each other.

"Maybe I should have taken one of the lower-level federal jobs I was offered when I graduated," I said. "Maybe I'd feel more normal."

"Not happening. You'd probably end up out of state, and none of those positions were what you wanted."

"Maybe not. But it feels so strange to be doing nothing."

"You have your own charity. And you just got out of your fellowship," he argued. "And you're always busy teaching survival classes."

"My survival skills are a hobby, Aiden. I want a real career where I can be making a difference. I'm going to keep volunteering, because every bit of experience I can get is valuable. But I want a job in conservation, even if I have to start at the bottom."

"You haven't really established yourself yet, Jade. Someday, you'll be so busy that you'll wish you could get a break. Don't rush things. You don't have to kill yourself anymore. Savor that for a while. Enjoy kicking back. It's something we never had when we were younger."

"You should talk," I told him soberly. "I don't see you and Seth slowing down."

"He's a slacker," Aiden answered. "If I let him slow down, he'd never pick up speed again."

I laughed. Aiden and Seth were close in age, and they were almost always together. But they loved to get underneath each other's skin. "How are things going?"

Our brother Seth had been in construction before we'd inherited a fortune. He'd done long, backbreaking days to help keep us all fed, and studied every single facet of the building-and-real-estate business along the way. Now, he and Aiden were buying huge lots of land to do their own building projects. As far as I could tell, they were becoming pretty well known as quality builders in a relatively short period of time.

"Good," he replied. "We're looking at some bigger projects now. We were hesitant to get in too deep until we got more experience under our belts. But things are hopping lately. For now, I think we're happy to be working toward becoming a housing giant. After that, we'll see."

I was so relieved to see my brothers content. The older three had worked so hard to help get me, Brooke, and Owen through college. They deserved every good thing that was happening for them right now.

"I'm glad," I told him quietly.

"Hey, are you up for pizza and a late-night movie? I don't feel like cooking."

"You never cook anyway," I reminded him. More often than not, he and Seth ended up at my house looking for food. I swore neither one of them ever went to the grocery store. "And I'd love to, but I can't. I have an overnight basic survival trip tomorrow. I have to be up really early."

Primitive survival was something I'd been passionate about for years, and I taught classes to share my knowledge. My overnights started early.

"Your loss," Aiden said. "I was going to offer to pay."

I laughed, just like my brother intended. "That sucks," I answered. "I really hate to miss free pizza."

Really, none of us knew quite how to act now that we had cash in our pockets. We could afford to eat anywhere we wanted to eat and we'd never miss the money.

"The being a billionaire thing is still weird, right?" I questioned him. "I still wake up every morning and open my eyes wondering if all of this was some kind of strange dream."

"And then you get out of bed and realize that you're in a beach house that's totally paid for." Aiden grinned as he stood up. "Weird in only the best of ways," he added as he grabbed his water. "Maybe I'll go and see what Noah and Seth are up to, since you're refusing my generous offer to buy you dinner. But I'm sure Noah won't go for taking any time off. He's working too damn much."

"Try to drag him away from his computer," I requested.

My eldest brother *did* work way too much. He always had. He'd been responsible for all of his younger siblings, so I didn't remember a time when Noah hadn't busted his butt to see us fed and healthy.

"I'll kick his ass," Aiden said with a nod as he opened the pool gate and let himself out.

I watched as my brother headed down the beach, obviously on his way to Noah's house, judging by the direction he'd gone.

I sighed when Aiden was out of sight, wondering if it was just me who couldn't manage to enjoy the money I'd inherited.

As of now, I seemed to be the only one still struggling with the fact that all of us had suddenly become very unlikely billionaires, and I just wasn't sure how to leave my old life behind.

CHAPTER 2

JADE

The next morning, I was still pondering how a family as poor as mine had suddenly come into massive amounts of money.

After getting up before sunrise, I'd thrown the things I'd need in a backpack and hit the road for the forty-minute drive into the backcountry.

My family story was convoluted, but also pretty simple. All of my full siblings and I shared a father with the powerful and super-rich Sinclair family from the East Coast. But we'd never known that until very recently.

I slowed down as I turned off the main highway.

I pulled onto the rough road to the small cabin on the property. There were enough bunk beds in the rustic structure for everybody, but students had the option of pitching tents or building their own shelters if they chose.

After I parked my Jeep, I unloaded some supplies and checked out the cabin. Although I encouraged foraging and trapping, I always made sure to have enough basic food so students didn't starve.

I sat on the wooden steps and took a deep breath, relaxing to the sounds of the birds and the feel of a light breeze that caressed my skin.

I opened the book I'd brought along, the latest from my favorite erotic romance writer. The reading material was one of my secret pleasures, maybe because I'd never been overwhelmed by lust for any man, but I loved to read about the possibility.

I was mostly a realist, but I loved the fantasy of some hot guy sweeping me off my feet.

Other than a boyfriend in college who had used me to help him get his degree and then disappeared after graduation without a word, I'd never been in a sexual relationship.

Honestly, my ex hadn't exactly rocked my world. But I liked to think that love and lust existed.

Brooke had always accused me of being a closet romantic. And maybe she was right. As a scientist, believing in soulmates, love, and unbridled lust didn't make much sense. But I couldn't stop myself from wanting to believe it was real anyway.

It had happened for my twin, and Brooke deserved the love she had with Liam. Her capacity to care about other people was endless.

A sigh escaped from my mouth as I started reading the scene I'd left off on the last time I'd picked up the book.

It was hot.

It was sensual.

And even though the male hero was an obnoxious alpha sometimes, I adored the way he wanted to give his woman everything and protect her from anything bad in the world, and how incredibly devoted he was to the woman he loved.

I paused after completing the scene, wondering if any male on Earth was really *that* involved in a female's pleasure. I knew the one guy in my life *hadn't* been. In fact, he got the deed over with as quickly as possible, which meant the moment *he'd* had his orgasm.

Doubtful most guys care if the female climaxes.

But the fantasy was something I didn't really want to give up.

So what if I could take care of myself?

There was some tiny place inside me that wanted a man who cared about . . . me.

"Hello, Jade," a smooth baritone said from above me, the deep voice startling me so much I instinctively slammed the book closed.

Even though I loved steamy romance, I didn't exactly broadcast it, except to my friends who read the same type of books.

Unfortunately, I'd gotten so lost in the hot fairy tale that I obviously hadn't heard my first student arrive.

I shaded my eyes and looked up, curious because the voice was familiar, but I was pretty sure that since I lusted after Eli Stone, I was hearing that whiskey-smooth baritone voice only in my imagination.

My heart skittered as I focused in on the face belonging to the sexy male voice.

It *was* Eli Stone, and I gaped at him like an idiot because I couldn't seem to reconcile *him* and being out in the *middle of nowhere*.

I scrambled to my feet, feeling at a disadvantage because I was so far below him. But the position change didn't help all that much. I was average height, and Eli Stone was all muscle—broad, tall, and pretty damn intimidating, even though he was casually dressed in jeans, a T-shirt that only showed how ripped he was, and a pair of hiking boots.

For just a moment, my eyes were drawn to the dark scrolls and sharp angles of the tribal tattoo that covered his left arm, ending at his wrist. The markings were a stark black against his tanned skin, and the ferociousness of the design left me speechless.

I wasn't into tats, and I'd seen Eli's in images many times, but there was something about those markings that made my heart lodge in my throat. They were fierce, but for some reason they only made me feel . . . sadness.

"What are you doing here?" I finally asked hesitantly as my gaze went back to his face.

He folded his muscular arms in front of him as he answered, "You didn't seem to want to come to me, so I'm coming to you. I'm your student for the next thirty-two hours or so, Jade."

I might not have been fond of Eli Stone, but his presence was still a little bit overwhelming.

Okay, maybe more than a *little bit*.

It had been so long since I'd seen Eli in person that I'd started to tell myself that I'd overestimated the tension that had flowed between us in his office.

But I really hadn't.

My body was taut just from being in close proximity to him, and the hypervigilant awareness I felt when I looked at him was very, very real.

The feelings were so powerful that I couldn't focus on anything else but *him*.

I didn't understand it.

But I *was* truly experiencing it.

The same awkward, potent attraction I'd fought in his office months ago.

I swallowed hard, my brain working to figure out exactly how I could get rid of Eli Stone before I made a complete and total fool of myself.

CHAPTER 3

ELI

Jade Sinclair looked like a deer in the headlights right now, and I could sense her panic.

Oddly, I didn't really want her to be intimidated by me. She sure as hell hadn't been when we'd met in my office.

Was it because we were alone in the middle of nowhere?

I suspected that wasn't the case, since she was out here routinely with people she didn't know.

Why in the fuck is she so afraid of me?

Granted, I'd lied to her when I told her in my office that I'd just wanted to see why she wanted to buy a piece of land that was worth almost nothing. But the truth was, I'd been intrigued by her reported character and skills for a long time.

One of my college acquaintances, a fellow adventure seeker, had taken one of Jade's advanced survival classes, and he'd told me about her.

She had a reputation in the San Diego area of being one of the best survivalists around.

When I'd gotten the opportunity to see her in person, I'd taken it.

Yes, I had been curious about why she wanted some worthless property. But that hadn't been my main motivation for wanting to meet her.

Unfortunately, I'd gotten caught up in a crisis right before her appointment time, so I'd *had* to make her wait.

I sure as hell hadn't *wanted* to put off the meeting, but I'd been wrestling with an issue that could cost a lot of people their jobs, so I hadn't had any choice.

I'd been relieved that she'd still been there when the crisis was over. Rather than discussing extreme survival with her, I'd ended up getting punched in the gut by the most beautiful, composed, outspoken, and entirely irresistible woman who had ever crossed my path.

She'd been nothing like I'd expected.

But everything I'd wanted just the same.

Since I was very much an amateur survivalist, I'd wondered if I could talk her into teaching me some of the things I didn't know. I had limited time, so I was going to try to convince her to teach me specifics to save time.

Unlike my acquaintance who had taken her class, I wasn't the least bit intimidated by the fact that a female knew more than I did about survival.

In fact, I'd been . . . intrigued.

Problem was, I hadn't planned on being attracted to her.

For some unknown reason, I wanted Jade Sinclair more than I'd ever wanted any other woman in my bed.

And I was determined to make it happen.

I had to have her to shake her out of my system. I was pretty damn tired of thinking about her so much that I couldn't sleep, couldn't keep my mind on work, and couldn't keep my dick deflated because she was becoming an obsession for me.

Unfortunately, getting her to spend time with me had been impossible. But I wasn't the type of man to admit defeat.

"You have to go," she finally said. "The class is full."

"I know," I answered. "I bought all of the spots over a month ago, plus I made a healthy donation to Save the Wildlife Corridors Fund that should go through today."

The shock on her face was nothing short of adorable. I knew I really should stop baiting her, but I couldn't help myself.

I wanted *her*.

And I never lost a deal or a competition that I really wanted to win.

I might have been born wealthy, but the empire I'd created after my father had passed away two years ago was all dogged determination. I never gave up when I knew I had to negotiate.

And there wasn't much I wasn't willing to put on the table to get a deal with Jade.

"I'm not doing this," she said, her chin going up. "You'd treat this class like a joke, and it's something that's important to me."

"Not even for a seven-figure donation to your charity?" I queried. Yeah, I kind of felt like a dick because I was trying to sway her with money. But her passion for wildlife was obviously a motivating factor for her, and I used any weaknesses I could find.

Her jaw dropped. "You gave that much to SWCF? Why?"

"Like you said, it's important to you."

"You could have just donated the land I wanted," she said suspiciously.

I shook my head regretfully. "I can't do that, Jade. And this isn't a joke. A friend took one of your advanced courses. He sang your praises, even though he was a little intimidated that a *woman* was teaching *him*. I was impressed. I could use more survival skills. I have a lot of hobbies that could leave me in a situation where I need the information you could teach me to survive."

Okay. Maybe that was just a little bit of bullshit, too, since I already had basic survival skills because of the extreme challenges I did on a regular basis. But I had to appeal to her sense of fairness somehow. And truthfully, Jade could teach me a lot more than I already knew.

Jade was intelligent and pretty much fearless, if the stories I'd heard were true.

Maybe she was a challenge, but it was more than that.

In the last several years, very little had intrigued me. But Jade did. And once my interest had been piqued, there had been no turning back.

I wanted to get to know her almost as much as I wanted to fuck her, which was new for me.

"Maybe I'm not all that good," she challenged. "But I'll teach you what I can, since you seem to need to be on television every damn week, so I assume you aren't going to stop doing ridiculous challenges anytime soon."

God, she's stubborn, but I kind of like that about her.

Jade was a woman with fire. She'd just never found anybody to stoke the flames, and I was determined to be the man who did.

She reminded me of a beautiful butterfly who was still struggling to get free of her cocoon. Obviously, she had some hang-ups, but I wasn't one to talk about that, since I was more fucked up than she could ever be.

"I don't *need* to be on television," I argued.

"For somebody who claims to not want attention, you certainly get plenty of it," she grumbled.

She was right. I did get international recognition. I took on some crazy things that most normal people would never volunteer to do. "It's always for a good cause. Most of the events I do are for charity."

She lifted an eyebrow. "And the rocketry company?"

"I do that for myself, and hopefully it will someday benefit future generations. But most of the things being done there now are research and development. We need better systems and equipment before we can do test runs."

I was determined not to lie to Jade again. I sensed that she'd appreciate honesty a whole lot more. Not that I was all that good at being candid, but there wasn't much I *wouldn't* do to get Jade in my bed.

Starting at the top of her dark head, my eyes roamed over her to try to figure what it was about this woman that had my dick tied in knots.

Jade had an earthy beauty that had captured me at first glance. Her mass of thick, dark hair was secured in a ponytail at the back of her head, but the simple style just made her blue eyes brighter. Her body was curvy, but extremely fit, a form I was quickly becoming drawn to much more than any thin model had ever tempted me.

I liked every single thing about her, even her inherent bullheadedness.

"I won't go easy on you," she warned.

Jesus! I was pretty sure that Jade could use me any way she wanted, and I found that rather perplexing.

I like control.

I need control.

Yet something about this particular woman had made me want to throw my desire for self-discipline out the damn window.

Keep the crazy going!

I grimaced as the words ran unwanted through my brain.

Maybe I *did* keep doing things that some people thought were the mad stunts of an out-of-control rich guy, but none of them knew just what I was made of underneath.

I was calculated.

I was careful.

I planned everything out in advance.

I really wasn't that big of a risk taker. I was just confident in what I could and couldn't do.

Maybe I needed that mastery of myself to balance out the crazy, and I did what I had to in order to stay sane.

"I wouldn't have it any other way," I told her.

"What survival experience do you have?"

I shrugged. "I survive in a world of business sharks."

She shook her head. "You know that's not what I meant."

"Not as much as you have," I confessed. "But I'm fairly handy to have around. I like working with my hands."

I saw a momentary hesitation flicker in her eyes, but she quickly masked it. Was she trying to decide if my words were actually an innuendo?

They were.

But she was obviously trying to give me a pass because she wasn't quite sure.

Behind Jade's brave front, I could see her vulnerability. She was probably much too naive in some ways, but I kind of liked that, too.

For some reason, I really hated the game we had to play right now. Although it worked well in business, I didn't like to see the wary look in her beautiful eyes when she glanced at me.

She was leery, and I couldn't say I blamed her. Honestly, my beautiful butterfly should be running as fast as she could to get away from me.

"We usually start with foraging and looking for anything that will be helpful as we locate a water source," she said carefully. "Did you bring the required items for the class?"

"Yep. Right here," I said as I picked up my backpack.

"Did you check it yourself?"

"No," I admitted. "My assistant got everything together for me. I was on a tight schedule."

"First rule of survival . . . check everything yourself. Nobody cares more about your life than you do."

Okay. I could live with that. I usually *did* check everything myself, because I was pretty much a perfectionist. Nobody cared about my conglomerate more than I did, so I stayed involved on all levels.

She continued, "Check your stuff and drop your backpack inside. Then we'll move out."

I went inside without an argument because what she said made perfect sense.

I smiled as I riffled through the items that had been prepared for me. Jade was bossy, and not unlike a diminutive, lovely drill sergeant when she was in her element.

I suddenly frowned as I realized even *that* made my dick hard.

CHAPTER 4

JADE

A few hours later, I began to realize that Eli had some standard skills.

He'd surveyed the landscape, using the basic signs to find a small stream where we'd filled up water bottles. We still had to boil the water, but Eli had managed to use his knowledge to find it.

Grudgingly, I had to admit that he really was interested in primitive survival.

I'd taught him some advanced skills, like how to make an underground still if he couldn't find an obvious source of water, and a few more ways to get drinking water in other climates.

He listened, which made my irritation with him fade away a little.

I'd expected him to scoff at everything I said or the things I tried to teach him. Instead, it had been exactly the opposite. Eli Stone seemed to suck up knowledge like a sponge, and he asked a lot of intelligent questions.

"What are these?" he asked as he stopped on the hiking path we'd been following back to camp.

I came to a halt next to him, reaching for his hand as he went to touch the small fruit bush. "Be careful," I warned as I gripped his fingers lightly. "These are really thorny. They're Natal plums, and the red fruit is edible, but the stems and leaves are toxic."

I let go of his hand and plucked one of the bright-red fruits from the tree. Pulling the knife I was carrying from its sheath on my belt, I carefully cut an edible portion and handed it to him.

The fact that he didn't hesitate to eat it, obviously trusting my knowledge without question, made me smile as I popped a piece of fruit between my own lips.

Rather than being a pain in my ass as I'd completely expected, Eli was a perfect student, and I'd been intrigued by the sensible facts he already had stored in his head. Not that I, in any way, thought he was a *nice guy*, but he wasn't as bad as I imagined him to be.

Unfortunately, that sexual tension in the air was ever-present, making it uncomfortable at times.

If I wasn't so damn attracted to him, I could probably enjoy his company.

"It tastes kind of like a cranberry," he said after he'd swallowed.

I nodded. "Sweet and sour."

He shot me a grin. "I find that flavor very tempting lately."

The flesh of the plum almost got caught in my throat, but I forced it down. I knew he was still playing his cat-and-mouse game, and that he was referring to me as the sweet and sour he found appealing. Unfortunately, the visual image his words conjured was automatic and vivid.

What would it be like to be devoured by Eli Stone?

I didn't *want* to have imaginary images of *that* unlikely occurrence flash through my brain, but I couldn't seem to control my errant thoughts.

I busied myself with cleaning my knife on nearby leaves and then shoved the blade back into its sheath. "We should get going," I said breathlessly.

"Wait," Eli said as he caught my upper arm to stop me, then pushed me gently against a nearby tree as he added, "I know you don't want to admit what we're both feeling right now, Jade. You don't want to talk about the fact that we're attracted to each other. But can't we just get it out there so you aren't so suspicious of my motives, Butterfly?"

"I'm not a butterfly," I said indignantly.

Did he really think I was a fragile, pretty living thing that had nothing better to do than flit from place to place?

"You *are* a butterfly," he disagreed. "And I think you're more than ready to emerge and fly free, but you haven't found your way out of your safe place yet."

God, it was almost terrifying that I pretty much felt the same way.

My body reacted immediately to being in such close proximity to his hot, hard, muscular body. My heart tripped as I looked up at him and saw the grim determination on his gorgeous face.

"I don't know what you mean," I said hesitantly, even though his words had struck a chord.

The last thing I wanted Eli to know was that my lust for him was nearly uncontrollable. So wild that I wanted to burst out of my *no one-night stands* position inside my cocoon and let him teach me everything I wanted to know about hot, sweaty, orgasmic sex.

He caged me in by putting a strong arm on each side of my body. "That's bullshit, Jade, and you know it. But if you won't talk about it, I will. I'm not afraid to admit that I want to fuck you. That there's not a single dirty thing I don't want to do with you. And it's driving me crazy."

The tension between us was electric, and the strain in his expression mirrored my own frustration.

I pushed against his enormous chest. "I don't just fuck any attractive man I see. That's not who I am."

He didn't budge, not even as I applied as much force as I was able to.

"Then what do you want, Jade?" he rasped. "The desire is there for both of us. I know damn well that I'm not feeling this all by myself."

"I want you," I blurted out as our eyes met and held. "You're an attractive guy. But I don't *like* you."

A flash of satisfaction moved across his face as he said, "You don't *know* me."

He was right. But *liking* Eli Stone was not an option for me. If I did, I'd be totally screwed. "I'm here to be your survival instructor. I don't have to like you."

He leaned forward and pressed his body against mine, his warm breath wafting across my ear as he said in a low, hungry tone, "You know what I think? I'm pretty sure you want a man who can instruct *you* for a change. I think you crave a guy who can actually make you submit and focus on nothing but pleasure."

"I don't!" I exclaimed, trying not to notice how good it felt when his teeth nipped at my ear and he soothed it with his tongue.

Heat raced between my thighs, and my heart was thundering as Eli moved back enough to look at me. "There's nothing wrong with wanting to be satisfied, Jade. You should demand it."

My mind was racing, trying to figure out how Eli could instinctively know what I wanted.

Maybe I did want to be with a man I didn't have to worry about intimidating.

And God, I really did want him to overwhelm me just like he was doing right now.

"Admit that you want me. I already know you do, but I want to hear it," he said in a persuasive tone.

I glared up at him even though my body was pleading for me to let Eli do any damn thing he wanted. "Dream on. I refuse to stroke your ego. I'm not going to give in to some kind of crazy lust I don't understand. It would never make me happy."

Okay. It might temporarily assuage my need, but I know I'd regret it if I let Eli get me into his bed for a one-nighter.

He grinned, a wicked, sultry smile that made my body scream for his touch. "I think it would make you *extremely* happy," he countered. "And the last thing I want you to stroke is my damn ego. I just want you to admit that you feel the same way I do. I know how to satisfy a woman, Jade. And I'd leave you so satiated that you'd never forget the experience. Give me a chance to show you how ecstatic you could be after you've been in my bed."

I opened my mouth to speak, but forgot every word I wanted to utter as Eli swooped down and captured my mouth.

For just a moment, I sank into the embrace that I craved, opening to him with a moan as his sensual kiss consumed me.

He'd been right.

I did want *this.*

I did want *him.*

I wanted him to take over so I could just feel the pleasure that was coursing through my body, enjoy the sensation of his mouth devouring mine.

Eli didn't do anything halfheartedly, and kissing was no exception. His embrace was breathtaking. And probably addictive.

He lifted his head, the embrace nothing more than a tease of what could be if I'd just say the word.

Yes.

"Let me go," I said as I pushed against his chest again. "I don't want to be controlled."

"I don't want to control you," he said huskily. "I want to be the man that you trust to take care of your needs."

He stepped back and I scrambled to the trail, with Eli right behind me.

My breathing was ragged, and I stopped for a moment to focus on getting air in and out of my lungs smoothly.

Eli stepped in front of me. "I don't want to hurt you, Jade. I never did. I feel the same things you do."

I looked up at him. "We don't have to act on the desire. What's the point? For just a little temporary relief? I can do that to myself."

Never in my life had I spoken to a guy about getting myself off, but Eli made me dare to say things I otherwise wouldn't.

Truthfully, I really didn't masturbate very much. I'd always been so exhausted from school and work that the time I got to myself was mostly for sleep.

"I'd like to watch," he said. "And then I could show you how down and dirty really *should* feel."

"You're assuming I don't know."

He shook his head. "I know you don't."

How in the hell does he know?

In reality, I had *no idea* how to do dirty things. But dammit, Eli tempted me to explore every one of those options.

My craving for him terrified me, and I wasn't sure why. Lots of women were perfectly capable of jumping into a man's bed just to satisfy an itch. And Eli Stone was much more than an irritation. He was a full-blown rash that I needed to scratch so hard that my skin would become raw.

"Drop it," I insisted. "I don't screw a guy and walk away. It's not my thing."

I turned and started making my way back to camp.

"I wouldn't let you walk away if you said yes, Jade," Eli warned as he fell into step beside me. "Neither one of us would be satisfied with a one-nighter. I'd need to be inside you over and over again before I could get you out of my system. One taste would never be enough for either one of us."

"I'm cutting this trip short right now if you don't stop," I said desperately.

Sweet baby Jesus! Eli needed to shut up before I did something I knew I'd regret.

I wasn't casual about sex.

I'd only been with one man.

And I knew I'd hate myself if I gave in to Eli Stone.

Problem was, I could also end up regretting not experiencing what this man could do to me, even if it just happened once.

Later, was I going to wish I'd felt what it was like to truly experience a mind-blowing orgasm like I instinctively knew Eli could give me?

He was silent as we walked, and I didn't trust myself to speak as we arrived back at camp.

By the time we'd hiked back, my brain was finally functional again.

Deep inside, I knew that I wasn't really afraid of having a fling with a man who could bring me nothing but pleasure.

But I was terrified that when it ended, I'd never be the same.

CHAPTER 5

JADE

Later that evening, I realized that there was one good thing about Eli buying out all my spots in the class: it left a ton of s'mores for us to eat without other students around.

Eli hadn't said another word about our personal dilemma, and I certainly hadn't encouraged him. In fact, I'd been relieved when he'd asked me about other methods of getting fire if there was no fire starter available.

I'd taught him how to make a bow drill and a hand drill. Surprisingly, he'd been able to get an ember with both of them. By the time we'd finished, it was dinnertime.

Since it was only an overnight beginner class, I'd pulled out the hot dogs and s'more fixings for dinner.

"Mine is done," I said as I watched my marshmallow turn a nice golden brown.

Eli chuckled as he handed over the graham crackers and chocolate. "You like to eat," he said with humor in his voice. "I think you're the most unusual woman I've ever met."

Yeah. Okay. So I *had* downed several hot dogs before I'd started in on the s'mores. I'd stopped counting how many I'd inhaled after the first few.

I turned my head and glared at him. We had a nice fire going, and I could see the glint of amusement in his eyes.

I shrugged. "I do like to eat. I've never been a woman who could exist on salad and water. And I burn a lot of calories. But what's so strange about that?"

Expertly, I slid the marshmallow between the crackers to melt the chocolate, giving the treat a good smash after it was in place.

"Nothing," he answered. "I like it because I love food myself. I guess I've just never found a woman who liked it as much as I do."

I moved from a kneeling position and plopped my ass on the ground beside him. I'd noticed that Eli could consume more food than I could, and that was saying something.

"I have four brothers," I said, like the statement explained everything. "They all love to eat, but there was a time when we didn't have enough money to feed all of us. Now that I have the money, I think I'm making up for lost time."

"What did you do when you couldn't all eat?" he asked.

"We survived. We rationed until we could get enough money to buy more groceries."

I took a big bite of my cooled-down s'more and closed my eyes as the sweet taste exploded on my tongue.

After being poor and hungry, I guess I appreciated food more than most people.

"What happened to your parents?" he said in a husky voice.

I opened my eyes, only to realize he was watching me intently. I swallowed before I answered, "My mom died when we were young. Noah was barely out of high school, but he still managed to keep us all together. We never really knew my father."

It was still hard to talk about the man who had sired us. We'd gotten to know our father through Evan and his siblings, and none of it was good. He'd been a mean, abusive man, and I actually felt lucky that he'd never been around much.

After I consumed the rest of my dessert, I licked my fingers until they weren't sticky anymore.

When I looked up, I could see the ravenous expression on Eli's face.

I held out the box of crackers and the chocolate. "Do you want more?"

He shook his head. "No."

The tension between us was still there, but the discomfort had eased for a while during the period that I was teaching him some new skills. Now it was back with a vengeance.

I looked away from him, unable to keep my eyes locked with his without falling under his seductive spell.

"So will you tell me about how you ended up sharing the same father with the East Coast Sinclairs now?" he asked huskily.

I let out a quiet sigh, glad he was at least trying to make normal conversation. "Only if you can keep it a secret. It's not like we're hiding it, or that it's in any way our fault, but gossip gets out of control. I already have every local guy in Citrus Beach trying to date me for my money, and some reporters have started hounding me for my story."

Now that Brooke had been home and found out about her inheritance, there wasn't much danger in telling Eli the truth. It had already leaked. But I didn't exactly want the whole world to know.

"I'd never repeat anything you tell me in confidence, Butterfly."

Strangely, I believed him. "It's not a pretty story. Martin Sinclair married his first wife and started a family on the East Coast. But he also married my mother after he already had a few children with his first wife."

"His first wife? He had two?"

"My father was a bigamist. I have no idea *why* he married my mother when he already had a wife. But I don't think my mother knew until he was already dead. She never told any of us the whole story before she passed away from an aggressive cancer."

"So none of you had any way of knowing that you shared blood with a rich and powerful family," he concluded.

I shook my head. "Not until I decided to do an ancestry DNA test. Since I love primitive survival, I wanted to see if I had any Native American blood. Really, we had no way of knowing my father's ancestral origins. So I was curious about our heritage on his side. There was a sale on the test, so I decided to go for it."

"So you matched with one of your half-siblings?"

"Evan. The oldest."

"I know him," Eli revealed. "Not well, but we've had some business dealings together. He is a cocky bastard, but not a bad guy."

I finally turned my head and smiled at him. "I think most of it is bravado with Evan. He put his DNA on the sites because he had suspicions that he might have more family in the world somewhere. When he settled his father's estate, he put a portion of our father's fortune aside and kept it growing in case we were ever found. That's a lot more than most rich people would ever do for their father's bastard kids."

"Agreed," Eli mused. "I guess he's a lot nicer than I thought."

"And look who's talking about being cocky," I said. "You're not exactly humble or considerate yourself. Is that a billionaire thing?"

"Is your conclusion because I left you waiting at my office?"

I nodded.

"Believe it or not, I'm actually very punctual. I have to keep a tight, organized schedule. But we had a crisis that day that forced me to push your appointment back. A lot of people were about to lose their jobs. Sometimes emergencies happen."

"Somebody could have told me," I argued.

"I told them not to. I was afraid you'd leave if you knew I was going to be tied up," he confessed with a mischievous grin.

Dammit. He was giving me that panty-dropping smile again, and damned if I wasn't ready to let go of my sensible cotton briefs because of it.

"I really want that land, Eli," I said in a hesitant voice, determined to change the subject. "I promise I'll take care of it."

I didn't want to get into an argument again about him leaving me in his waiting room for an hour. I had a feeling he was sincere about what held him up, and if he really had to save jobs, it was well worth the wait I'd had to deal with while he did it.

But I had my opportunity to try to convince him to part with the backcountry property I wanted, and I was going to take my best shot.

As a pained expression passed over his face, I was almost sorry I'd started up the conversation again. "I can't, Jade," he answered sternly.

"Why?"

"It's personal," he grumbled. "And I still don't entirely understand why *you* want it."

I took a deep breath. "Like I said, it's an important wildlife corridor. If the land gets developed someday, the wildlife could end up trapped, and they could start inbreeding because they don't have access to a wider genetic pool. Tons of species use that passage to expand their territory, and the backcountry is important to me. I grew up exploring there. It's what got me interested in ecology and wildlife in the first place."

He was quiet for a minute before he asked, "Inbreeding? Like the mountain lions in Santa Monica?"

I was surprised he'd even paid attention to that, or knew about it. Most people outside the wildlife field weren't aware of it. "That's a very good example. Everything built up around the mountain lions, and they had no open corridors, so they were essentially trapped. Inbreeding can lead to congenital defects, and it threatens the entire population there. If there's no genetic diversity, they'll likely become extinct in that area."

"I'll protect it, Jade. I'll never develop it," he answered hoarsely. "But I can't sell."

He sounded so troubled that I dropped the subject. "Okay."

I wanted to push him for the reasons why he'd refused to sell, but the desperate tone of his voice told me it was something highly personal.

We sat in silence for a few minutes, but it wasn't an uneasy quiet.

Finally, I asked, "Is there anything else you'd like to learn before we head out tomorrow?"

"A lot of things, actually," he said in an earnest tone. "I'd like to pick your brain some more. You're as intelligent as you are beautiful."

"I wish you'd stop saying things like that," I blurted out.

"Why?"

"Because you've known far more attractive women, so it makes me uncomfortable. I'm okay with who I am, so I don't need fake compliments."

"How do you know that you aren't the sexiest woman I've ever seen?"

I rolled my eyes, but he probably couldn't see me since I was staring into the fire. "The A-list actress and the two supermodels you dated are pretty much a dead giveaway."

"I'm not with *them* anymore. I'm with *you*," he stated simply. "Did somebody do a number on you, Jade? Because it sounds to me like someone made you feel like you aren't perfect, which you are, whether you see it or not."

"I've always been a geek," I shared. "In high school, I was the girl every guy avoided because I was a tomboy. But I didn't really care all that much. I was happier just being outside alone."

"What about college?"

I shrugged. "I was still a geek. I had one boyfriend, and he ended up leaving me without a word after I helped him through his master's degree."

"He was probably intimidated by you, and he's a total idiot if he didn't hang on to you. His loss; my gain."

What my brother Aiden had said about insecure guys just yesterday popped into my head. "I'm not really intimidating."

"You are," he countered. "But I personally get turned on by a woman who can handle a knife better than I can."

A laugh escaped my mouth. "You're crazy."

"At least I'm honest," he said.

I stood up. "I think I'd better get to bed. Are you pitching a tent, or do you want a bunk?"

My conversation with Eli was getting dangerous. If I didn't stop it now, I might start believing that he actually *did* see me as more attractive than the women he'd dated, and just the thought of that was ludicrous.

Eli rose and blocked my way to the cabin. "Hey," he said in a low, fierce tone. "Don't ever let anybody make you feel like you aren't a woman worth fucking fighting for. Your ex was an idiot, but that's about him, not you."

I felt tears start to pool in my eyes, but I blinked them away. "It's not just that," I said quietly. "What guy wants a woman who would rather eat like a pig or spend the day outside instead of dressing up and going out to a club or something?"

Eli stepped forward and dropped a kiss on my forehead. "Me," he said gruffly. "And I'll take a bunk. It's too damn cold to sleep outside."

I nodded and led the way inside, trying to ignore that nearly unstoppable desire to throw myself into his arms and beg him to give me the mother of all orgasms.

For some insane reason, Eli Stone really did want me.

And I was getting pretty tired of fighting my own insane attraction to him.

CHAPTER 6

Jade

"I don't really know *how* to be a billionaire," I confessed quietly into the darkness.

Eli and I had settled in, and he was in the bunk bed above me. I'm not sure why I'd uttered the words, but talking to the dark seemed safe.

And I couldn't sleep, an affliction that rarely happened to me.

I had no idea whether or not he was still awake, and I almost hoped he hadn't heard my pathetic comment. It was kind of stupid. If my biggest problem was adjusting to having money, I was pretty sure most people would love to be in my shoes.

"People think having a lot of money is easy, but it really isn't," Eli answered in a husky voice. "From now on, you're always going to wonder what somebody wants from you when you meet anybody new. And if you put yourself in the social circle of ultrawealthy people, you'll never have your privacy. Once you get known, you'll always be in the public eye. There's not a lot of privacy sometimes. On the other hand, there are lots of benefits."

His voice was low and smooth, and I was relieved that he didn't laugh at me for saying something silly. Eli actually sounded like he understood me to some extent.

"What benefits? Being able to buy things?" I asked earnestly.

He chuckled. "There's *definitely* that. But it could also open doors to things you've never been able to do before. Money can be a trap or freedom. It is what you make of it. And you can do a hell of a lot of good. Billionaires can be excellent fund-raisers and benefactors to charities if they choose to be."

I already knew that Eli was a huge philanthropist. All of the causes he donated to came up frequently in his interviews.

"I'd like that," I murmured. "I have my own charity, but there are others that I'd like to work with, too. I know my twin sister is taking an active role in fund-raising."

"You have a twin?" he asked hoarsely, sounding surprised.

"Her name is Brooke. She married a guy in Maine, and I really miss her. I'm happy for her, but having her so far away is like losing my right arm. There's a twin bond that will never go away."

"You're lonely?" he probed. "That's completely understandable, especially now. You were thrown into a whole new reality, and she's not around for you to work things out together."

"I just feel like a part of me is missing," I shared. "Brooke was always my best friend."

"Keep busy," he suggested. "Eventually, you'll find your own way."

"So maybe I just need to try to experience new things?"

"You definitely should," he agreed. "Have you ever done an African safari? You love wildlife, and it's pretty amazing."

"No." Seeing places and traveling to experience the wildlife in other countries *was* pretty appealing. I'd done plenty of studies on African wildlife, but most of it was genetic, and I'd only observed the animals in captivity. To see them running in the wild would be extraordinary.

"Australia? The animals there are pretty unique."

"No."

"South America? China? Europe? Canada?"

"Nope. I've never been in *any* foreign country," I admitted.

Honestly, maybe I hadn't thought about foreign travel because I really didn't want to go alone. If I got a job abroad, it would be different. I'd be working in another country. But just to see the sights, it would suck not to have anybody to share it with. And now that Brooke was married and across the country, I had no idea who would want to go with me. My friends all had full-time, busy jobs.

"You have to start thinking like a billionaire, Jade," he said with obvious amusement. "I know you love food. Have you hit any of the great restaurants in San Diego?"

Dinner for one? That would be awkward.

"No. But you own most of them. So I can see why you've been to every one of them. The only place of yours that I've tried is the spot we celebrated Brooke's engagement. I saw you there."

"You know I saw you, too," he said. "I made sure dinner was on the house for your whole party before I left."

"Noah didn't tell me that," I said. "Why did you do it? It's not like my family doesn't have the money now."

"I could tell you were celebrating. I wanted to do it. Besides, your brother Noah just took the amount of the bill and tipped his waitress with it. I had one very happy waitress that night. I doubt that story will ever stop circulating around the place." He paused before he added, "And I go to places I don't own. I told you that I love food."

I wasn't surprised that my eldest brother had given the waitress a monstrous tip, but I felt a little guilty about the fact that I hadn't exactly had kind thoughts about Eli that night. He'd actually done something really thoughtful.

"I'm not much of a socializer," I said, feeling defeated. "And going to dinner in nice places alone isn't all that much fun."

"You could have gone with me," he reminded me. "Fuck knows I've offered over and over again."

"I didn't like you," I said bluntly.

"You don't *know* me," he argued. "And you have no reason to *dislike* me."

I stared into the darkness for a few minutes, contemplating his statement.

He'd pretty much cleared up why he'd left me waiting in his office. He didn't want to sell the land I wanted, but it wasn't like he had to do anything he didn't want to do. He said he had his reasons, and the acreage in the backcountry obviously had some deep meaning to him personally. And I could hardly fault him because he had extreme hobbies. It was his life. He had a right to do whatever he wanted.

"You're right," I finally muttered. "We don't have much in common, but that's no reason to *dislike* you."

"You're attracted to me, and you don't like *that*," he said. "Do I scare you, Jade?"

"Sometimes," I confessed, the total darkness making me braver.

"Why?"

Because every time I see you, I get mesmerized. I want to crawl up your gorgeous body and ease the painful ache I have every time you're near me.

"Because I don't like losing control," I finally answered. "I'm not the type of woman who makes any man drool. Brooke was always the more feminine one. I was a tomboy, remember?"

"Maybe you like being outdoors, but you're gorgeous, Jade. You have a natural beauty that would knock some guys on their asses."

"Like you?"

"Especially me," he confessed. "You're so connected with nature and the wildlife you're fighting to protect. I love the way you handle an axe, and I'm in awe that you can identify nearly any plant. It makes you pretty irresistible."

I couldn't help it. I laughed out loud. "Eli, there aren't a whole lot of men who find a dirt-smudged woman with no makeup, and who chronically has bad-hair days, all that pretty."

"Not another comment about how you look, or I swear I'll swing down into your bed and make you realize just how damn fuckable you really are," he growled.

Every part of me wanted to say something that would make Eli bring his ripped body into my bed, but I still had a tiny portion of common sense, so I stayed quiet for a moment before I simply answered, "Okay. I'll stop."

"Damn!" he said hoarsely.

He sounded so disappointed that I smiled into the darkness and changed the subject. "So how did you get so comfortable with being a celebrity?"

"I'm *not* a celebrity," he said. "I was born rich. So I pretty much grew up in a privileged world. But I never really wanted to be noticed. It just . . . happened."

I rolled my eyes, even though he couldn't see me. "Please. Every news organization loves to show you doing your extreme hobbies, or talk about how you're one of the most eligible bachelors in the world. You're not exactly what I'd call a low-profile billionaire."

"Now I want to be noticed sometimes, especially when I'm raising funds for charity."

I supposed getting attention for his causes was probably worth being in the public eye. "Do you like the publicity?"

"You probably won't believe me, but I actually don't. I'm a private kind of guy. But I'm willing to sacrifice some of my privacy for a good cause. Sometimes I have to keep the crazy going."

Keep the crazy going?

It was an interesting way to refer to his insane hobbies and fund-raising.

He hesitated before he said, "You'll get used to having money, Jade. It doesn't change who you are, and once you start enjoying the benefits of being a billionaire, you just might find out it isn't so bad."

"I'd like to travel," I mused. "And I do like raising money for my charity. I wouldn't mind doing as much as I can for other fund-raisers."

"I can teach you what billionaires can do for fun. And then I can show you how we can make a difference in the world. Give me some of your time, and I promise that I'll make you feel differently about having money," he said gruffly.

"By taking me to dinner in a nice place?" I asked curiously. There was something very appealing about having someone to show me the billionaire ropes, because I was clueless as to how I could become a good philanthropist.

"Among other things," he answered. "Give me ten days, Jade. I can take that much time off. I might have emergencies come up, but I'll otherwise be at your disposal. I can help you get used to being rich, and prove that it doesn't change you."

My heart tripped. I couldn't imagine spending every single day with Eli for over a week. But I would be lying if I said I wasn't tempted. Eli seemed to understand my fears about the money, and I could talk to him. "I have classes," I argued.

"No, you don't," he replied smugly. "I bought them all out for the next month. I was hoping you'd agree to spend some time with me."

"I know I had some people who wanted to sign up."

"Classes were already booked. Those potential students got pushed to the following month."

"How in the world did that happen? How did you manage to buy out all the classes?"

"I have a lot of friends in San Diego," he answered. "And I was desperate."

My schedule was put together by some of the rec centers who recommended my classes. So it irritated the hell out of me that somebody had just . . . fixed it for Eli.

There was part of me that was annoyed that he'd high-handedly stripped me of the ability to teach classes for a month, but there was a soft spot inside me because Eli was trying so damn hard.

And really, I didn't have much desire to fight him. I wanted to get to know him. He did some great things for charity, and I wanted to be part of that. And I had the chance to work with a man who had grown up rich. If anybody knew the ins and outs of being a billionaire, he did. "Are you going to try to kiss me again?"

"Undoubtedly," he said firmly.

I wasn't sure whether the thought terrified me, or if I was secretly glad.

"I suppose you did donate a lot of money to my charity," I mused.

"Don't agree because of that. I wanted to donate," he said huskily. "Do it because you want to or not at all. I donate millions to charity, but I'll make you a deal."

"What?" I answered in a breathless voice.

"Do the days with me, and on the last day I'll throw a fund-raising event for SWCF. I'll get every person I know with money to attend. You'll raise a fortune for your nonprofit, and I'll teach you how to keep doing it. I'll introduce you to every influential person I know."

The thought of learning to do charity fund-raising from Eli was a dream come true. But being with him for over a week was even more tempting. "I'd like to," I admitted.

"But? I definitely hear a hesitation. What is it, Jade?"

"I'm not sure what your motivation is," I admitted. "Are you trying to get me into your bed?"

"Yes," he said bluntly. "But I'd really like to get to know you. I haven't had any real time off in a long time. And I'd like to spend those days with you."

"What are we going to do?" I asked nervously.

"I get to arrange the days," he insisted.

"I don't like surprises," I muttered.

"You'll learn to love them," he countered.

I knew it was way past time I got more into the human world. I'd spent too much time in the backcountry conducting research. I'd been isolated, and I was starting to get lonely, especially with my twin across the country.

"Okay. I'm not going to be seduced," I said firmly. "But I think I'd like to be your friend."

"We'll see," Eli said mysteriously. "I very much doubt we can be friends, Butterfly. We're too attracted to each other. And I don't really do girlfriends or commitment. I have . . . arrangements."

I already knew that about him, but hearing the words come from him directly made me sad. At times, he could be a really nice guy. So I was having a hard time figuring out why he could also be a jerk.

Something is haunting him.

Brooke would say that it was my closet romantic, thinking that Eli was better than he really was, but I just had a weird sense that he wasn't always showing his true face. I'd seen it in his interview, and I felt it even stronger now that I'd spent some time with him.

"I'm not going to give in on the sex thing, so you're wasting your time if that's all you want."

"Spending time with you would never be a waste, whether we burn up the sheets or not."

His comment silenced me momentarily because he sounded so sincere. "I want to spend time with you, too, Eli. But I don't want to sleep with you. I'm a commitment type of woman, and if I have sex with somebody, I'd at least like that option to be open."

My statement was a little white lie, a comment that was much more about convincing myself I didn't want him to fuck me than letting him know how I felt. But most of it was honest. I did want to have a committed relationship if the right guy came along.

"Let's just spend the time together and see what happens," he suggested.

I already knew what would happen. I'd be hot and bothered every moment we were together. I was seriously starting to wonder if I had masochistic tendencies.

"Did you hope I'd end up giving in tonight?" I asked curiously.

"Yep. But I did accomplish one thing," he said thoughtfully.

"What?"

"I have your body underneath mine, even if it isn't exactly how I'd planned it."

I snorted. My bunk bed *was* underneath his. "You're crazy," I told him.

"I have been since I met you," he agreed readily.

I rolled on my side with a long sigh. Eli had a quirky sense of humor that I was quickly beginning to like. And I was slowly getting used to his sexual innuendos.

I could handle them in the dark with him in another bed.

But I wasn't too certain I'd do as well if I could see him.

"Good night, Eli," I said sleepily.

"Sweet dreams, Butterfly."

I was asleep moments later, and I was pretty sure I conked out with a smile on my face.

For some reason, it never occurred to me that I should be wary of sleeping in the same cabin with a guy who wanted my body.

As long as I professed to be unwilling, I knew I was safe.

CHAPTER 7

JADE

"Sounds like you had fun," I said to my twin sister, Brooke, as we spoke on the phone the following evening.

My sister's husband, Liam, had gotten a manager for his restaurant in Maine, and he and Brooke were traveling a lot. She'd just arrived home from a second honeymoon, even though they'd only been back from their first one a few days before the second one had taken place.

I was happy for her. She was in love and having the time of her life. Was it awful that talking to her sometimes made me feel incredibly lonely?

"The Caribbean was amazing," Brooke answered. "You should go. You'd love it."

"I have a beach right here," I told her good-humoredly. "And I feel pretty damn lucky to live right on it now."

"It's still weird, right?" Brooke asked. "The money thing. We spent so many years being poor. *Really* poor. And now the world is wide open for all of us."

"I'm still not used to it," I confessed. "I know there are so many great things I could do, and so many experiences I could have. But I feel paralyzed by the money. I'm not quite sure where I should go from here. Until recently, my fellowship kept me so busy that I didn't have time to think about it. But now that I'm done, I have a lot of time to feel terrified and guilty."

"Sudden Wealth Syndrome," Brooke said thoughtfully. "I was pretty confused at first, too. But Liam helps me stay grounded."

"Is that really a thing?" I asked.

"Of course," Brooke replied. "It's something that can happen to anyone who suddenly comes into money—like lottery winners, athletes, movie stars, and people who get a large inheritance like we did. I researched it a lot after I found out about the money. I didn't understand why I wasn't ecstatic about having so much money. I guess I felt like I didn't deserve it. Google it. It isn't unusual to feel unworthy, guilty, isolated, and terrified about what to do with the money."

Brooke had never really talked about questioning her own sudden wealth. She'd been way too happy about her impending marriage to the man of her dreams.

"I feel that way, too," I confided. "But who can I really talk to about it? It seems ridiculous to confide in any of my friends. Who is going to understand that I'm freaked out by inheriting billions?"

"And I don't suppose our brothers are really feeling guilty," Brooke commented drily.

"Not a bit. They're all planning their futures and working on building their own empires. I don't think they've ever given it a second thought. I wish I could feel the same way and suddenly figure out what I want to do with my life, just like our brothers did. But I feel guilty and isolated now."

The few friends I had were working their asses off to succeed. I'd been in their shoes just a short time ago, but I didn't quite fit into that world now. I felt like they'd pretty much abandoned me since I'd suddenly become wealthy. It was like they didn't think I was one of them anymore.

And maybe I wasn't.

But I didn't know where else I belonged.

It wasn't like I'd really changed.

I was the same geek, who just happened to have an overinflated bank account now.

"It will just take time, Jade," Brooke said in a soothing voice. "You don't have to make any big decisions until you're ready. You're doing the things you love, and you're finished with your education. Just keep doing what you're doing. If your friends abandoned you, make new friends."

Brooke didn't really understand that I didn't make friends that easily. But I decided not to point that out to her.

"I've sent out a ton of résumés and applications, but people aren't exactly breaking down my door to hire me."

"Give yourself a break," Brooke answered, sounding exasperated. "You busted your rear for years to get through school, and you worked some of the world's worst jobs just to get through your doctorate. Keep putting in applications and your résumé for the positions you want. In the meantime, enjoy your time without having to worry where your next meal is coming from."

"I want to take over my own finances and investments, but I'm scared," I shared with my twin. "Evan has been helping me, and he's pretty much managing my portfolio. But I want to be involved. I'm just afraid I'll screw everything up."

"I know. I felt that way, too. But Liam is an incredible investor, and he's been reassuring me. Plus, I have the financial education to figure it all out."

"No rich guy in sight for me right now," I joked lightly. "Just a lot of local guys who want to date my money."

Brooke made a disgusted sound. "Ignore those jerks. You need to get into the big city more. You've always been too smart for any of the local guys."

I smiled. "I guess you were, too, since you had to go across the country to find Liam."

"He was worth it," she said firmly. "There's somebody out there for you, too, Jade. You just have to find him. Or he has to find you."

"Well, until he shows up, maybe Eli can help me," I said thoughtfully.

"Eli? You mean Eli Stone? The guy you can't stand?" Brooke probed.

I hadn't shared a lot with Brooke about Eli in the beginning, but after she'd gotten married, I hadn't hidden anything from her.

"He bought out all of my survival classes so he could see me. What guy does that, Brooke?"

"I think a man who really, really likes you and doesn't have a chance of you returning his phone calls," Brooke teased.

"I don't think he really likes me all that much. He just wants to screw me. We have this weird attraction to each other that I can't explain."

Brooke laughed. "Yeah. That's how it was with Liam. And look how *that* turned out."

"I found out he wasn't really all that bad," I said. "I actually like his sense of humor, but he's a little . . . intense. But I finally decided to go out with him. I wouldn't mind being his friend."

"So where is he taking you?" Brooke asked excitedly.

"I have no idea. I'm spending ten days with him. Every day will be a surprise. When our ten days are over, he's doing a fund-raiser for SWCF."

"Does this ten-day deal include nights, too?" she asked.

I knew exactly what she meant. "No."

"But he definitely likes you," Brooke observed. "Look at everything he's doing to get your attention."

"Oh, he *has* my attention," I answered. "I just don't understand why he's going to so much trouble for me. We've seen the kind of women he dates, Brooke. All of them are gorgeous and successful."

"You're gorgeous and successful, too," she said firmly.

"I'm not in the same league as the women he dates, and you know it."

"I love you dearly, Jade, but you need to loosen up. You have a rich, sinfully delicious man who wants to spend time with you. Just let go and have some fun."

"I'm really attracted to him," I said unhappily.

"What's wrong with that? It will make every day a lot more exciting. I get that you don't know if he's the right guy for you, but you'll never know until you hang out with him and get to know him. What we know about him is just a persona, an image created by the media. Find out who he *really* is. If he's willing to arrange a fund-raiser for your charity, he obviously knows how much it means to you, and he's willing to help."

I understood what she meant. Our Sinclair half brothers and cousins had been rich since birth. Every one of them had a media image, but that wasn't who they really were. For example, Evan was thought to be a complete prick. But we'd all come to know the real Evan, and he was nothing like the way he was portrayed.

"He wants to help me get comfortable with my money because he knows it kind of terrifies me. At least, that's what he told me. He wants to show me how to live in that world and like it."

"Perfect," Brooke replied. "And at least you know he definitely isn't after your money."

I smiled. "That's one thing I don't have to worry about. Maybe that's why it's so appealing. But don't start thinking this is going to be a long-term thing. I'm not going to end up married to Eli Stone. He's not into commitments. I'm just . . . experimenting. I'm hoping maybe I can learn some things from him. I'd love to have his expertise in fund-raising."

"You want his hot, ripped, gorgeous body, even with the tattoos," she contradicted me.

"I'm not after his body," I muttered. "But the tats are actually kind of mesmerizing in person."

"Come on, Jade. You're talking to your twin. You want *more* than just his brain."

"Who wouldn't?" I asked her. "Brooke, you know what he looks like. And take it from me, he's even hotter up close and personal."

"But chemistry will only carry you so far," she warned. "No matter how good he looks, the attraction will wear off if you don't like him."

"That's the problem," I replied. "I do like him. He's kind of pushy and arrogant, but he seems like a decent guy once you get past all that arrogance."

"Don't sell yourself short, Jade," Brooke said softly. "You have a lot to offer any guy. Even a smoking-hot billionaire."

"I hate feeling so damn inadequate," I said. "I never felt this way when I was poor. I knew who I was and what I wanted to be. I was going to be a researcher and discover ways to keep some species from going extinct. But then the money happened, and none of the jobs I really wanted have come my way. Being rich allowed me to refuse the positions I didn't want, and I have no desire to teach in a classroom. I'd go crazy, Brooke."

"You would," she agreed. "You wouldn't have been happy. And there's nothing wrong with waiting to figure out what you want. There're no positions you want in San Diego?"

"There are plenty of them," I told her. "But none that are available right now."

I'd completed a postdoc fellowship studying the genomes that were vulnerable to extinction in large mammals. I'd produced a lot of published studies that had gotten great responses, but a position to continue my studies had never panned out.

"I'm sorry, Jade," Brooke responded. "I know how much you want to keep researching, but it might take some time."

"It seems I have plenty of that," I teased halfheartedly.

"You can pretty much do whatever you want," she answered.

I was starting to feel bad because I was such a downer for Brooke when she was so happy. "I'll be patient. At least I don't have to just take something in order to work, thanks to our windfall. I'll keep volunteering so I can network more."

"You deserve this rest, Jade. Remember that," Brooke said adamantly. "We went hungry as kids, and every one of us worked to bring in money as soon as we were old enough. You busted your ass to get somewhere. It doesn't matter that you got lucky with the money. You'll be successful because you've always been driven. Maybe none of us expected to end up quite this rich, but we've worked hard since we were kids. Martin Sinclair *was* our father, and he left our mother destitute while he lived a life of gluttony. Bastard children or not, we deserve to join the rest of our family and to get back what we never had when we were younger."

I sighed. "Sometimes I wish the money would just go away and I could go back to how things were before. I'd probably be working in a government job of some kind by now. I would have found a full-time gig as soon as I could, even if it wasn't in my area of interest or expertise. But now I feel like I'm in limbo."

"It will go away, Jade," Brooke said. "I know it all seems weird right now, but you'll figure it all out in time. Don't push yourself too hard. Evan will handle your portfolio as long as you want."

"I know. But I feel like I should be doing more than I am right now."

"Because we're all used to being so busy we don't have time to think," Brooke explained. "But that's never been healthy for any of us. We all need some balance. Have fun with Eli. And if you sleep with him, I need to know immediately," she teased.

"I'm not going to go to bed with him," I said hastily. "I guess I'm just hoping for some enlightenment. Eli has been rich his entire life, and he got a whole lot richer after his father passed away. He's a good businessman."

"He's a gorgeous billionaire," she corrected. "And I think you want more than an educational experience. I'll be dying to find out how it's going."

"I'll keep you posted," I promised.

"Are you going to be okay?" Brooke asked. "Do you want me to fly home so we can spend some time together?"

"That would make Liam my enemy," I joked. "No, thanks. I like my new brother-in-law. And I'll be fine. I'm just a little bit overwhelmed, but I'll work it out."

"You know that I'm always going to be there for you, right? Even though I'm married now, I'm still your twin sister."

I blinked back the tears that sprang to my eyes.

Brooke might be far away, but our twin bond was ever-present. "Thanks. Maybe I needed to hear that. But I'll be fine."

I had no doubt that if Brooke thought I needed her, she'd drop everything to be here. It was a comforting thought. But I wasn't about to drag her away from her new husband.

"I love you," Brooke said tearfully.

"I love you, too," I answered as a tear hit my cheek.

"Call me," she insisted. "I have to know how your experiment is working out."

We talked for a few more minutes, and then hung up with the promise to call each other more often.

I relaxed as I hung up the phone. I'd been missing Brooke, and because of her travels, we hadn't had a lot of time to talk. But I should have realized that none of my siblings, no matter how busy, were ever going to forget how much we meant to each other.

We'd all grown up as a group, fought for each other, and because we were all together, we flourished as people despite being poor.

My mood elevated after my short pep talk, and I rose from my couch to go put things together for the morning. Eli had texted me to let me know that I needed to bring a swimsuit and dry clothing.

My heart skittered as I pictured his face the morning after I'd practically blabbed out every emotion I was feeling into the darkness the night before.

His gray eyes had remained fixed on me until we'd departed from the cabin, but he hadn't appeared to get any less fierce since hearing about all my insecurities. In fact, I sensed that he somehow wanted to protect me from something.

Unfortunately, the thing I actually needed to be shielded from was him.

CHAPTER 8

Jade

I was gathering up my backpack the next morning when I heard my doorbell ring.

A quick glance at the clock confirmed that Eli was right on time.

I smiled as I realized that he was probably trying to prove that he didn't *always* leave people cooling their heels because of him.

Picking up my things, I made my way to the door, trying not to admit that I was curious about what we were doing for the day.

But I was pretty unsuccessful.

I'd worn my swimsuit underneath my jeans and T-shirt, and I had clean clothes in my pack. So yeah, I had to assume that we were doing something near the water, but that wasn't really a stretch since we lived on the coast.

Honestly, I *was* excited. I'd never really had much as far as adventures in my life. And I'd been too caught up in fear and guilt after I'd inherited a pile of money to do much with the enormous amount of wealth I'd inherited. Maybe because I'd been too damn scared to touch it.

Sure, I'd bought a beachfront home. But it was modest for a beach house, a two-bedroom waterfront cottage with a pool that I absolutely adored. Compared to my brothers' mansions down the beach, my place looked like a second-rate condo.

I stopped as I approached the screen door that led out onto my deck, my eyes drawn to one of the most adorable dogs I'd ever seen.

Soulful brown eyes stared at me from outside, and my heart melted. The dog was a shaggy beast. He looked like a mix that had the markings of a shepherd, but floppy ears like another breed entirely.

He might have been enormous, but his tail was wagging, and his eyes suckered me in even after I opened the door.

"Hey, buddy. Where did you come from?" I put my hand out so he could sniff it.

"He's mine," a deep voice said from beyond the deck. As Eli came up the stairs and into my vision, he had a grin on his face. "He knows how to ring doorbells as long as they're low enough for him to reach. I sent him ahead so I'd be exactly on time."

The pup nuzzled my hand and I crouched down to give him the love he wanted.

"He *cannot* ring the doorbell," I said in disbelief.

"He did," Eli argued. "Charlie . . . go ring," he commanded.

The dog actually stopped soaking up affection from me and put his paws on the side of the house before he smacked one of them against the doorbell.

I gaped at Eli as the doorbell chimed.

At Eli's signal, the canine dropped all four paws onto the deck again.

"That's incredible," I said in awe as I resumed petting the dog.

"I hope you don't mind," Eli said. "Charlie hates to be left out. I take him along whenever I can. He was a mutt rescue that was abused, and he likes to be with me."

My heart warmed as I realized that Eli seemed completely devoted to his pet's welfare, and that he'd actually adopted from an animal shelter instead of getting some fancy purebred.

I stepped back and motioned for both of them to come in. "I don't mind at all. I love dogs. But I've never been able to afford to have one of my own. Well, until now."

I hadn't even considered getting myself a pet. Maybe because I was gone so much overnight. Or possibly due to my freaky Sudden Wealth Syndrome or whatever it was that kept me scared of spending any of my inheritance.

But thinking about it, maybe a pet *would* help me feel less isolated.

"We can't stay here long," Eli warned. "Our ride is coming."

"Coffee?" I asked as I entered the kitchen and Eli took a seat at the breakfast bar.

"Yeah. I always have time for *that*," he answered good-naturedly.

"How did you get here if you don't have a ride?" I asked as I poured us each a mug of coffee.

"I have a car, but I'm staying right next door during my little vacation," he answered as he motioned for Charlie to lie down. The dog obeyed immediately.

My head shot up. "Next door. You mean here? In Citrus Beach?"

He gave me that panty-dropping smile that got me every time as he said, "I live in San Diego. I didn't want to bother with the traffic and drive every day, and the house next door was for sale, so I bought it. I just drove up this morning. It was a vacation rental, so it came completely furnished."

I poked a thumb to my right. "That house?" I remembered that the mansion was on the market.

He nodded as he motioned away the cream and sugar and took the black coffee from me.

I added cream and sweetener to my own mug as I said, "That place is almost brand-new, and it's enormous."

He shrugged his broad shoulders. "It's not that big. Six bedrooms, maybe. I didn't really have time to look."

Maybe I was having problems processing the fact that Eli had just up and bought the place next door to me, but I couldn't stop staring at him in disbelief.

Not that he was at all hard to look at. Dressed in a pair of dark jeans and a T-shirt, he looked so damn good that I could hardly force myself to look away.

"Who does that?" I asked, dumbfounded. "Who just buys a house sight unseen?"

He took a slug of coffee before he answered. "To be honest, I pretty much buy every home I have without seeing it. I have employees who handle the details."

"How many homes do you have?" I asked nervously, almost afraid to hear his answer.

"I'm not sure," he answered. "I lost track. But they're all good investments. I have a few I haven't had a chance to stay in yet, but it's convenient to have homes everywhere."

I swallowed hard as I stared at him. Granted, I was *barely* a billionaire and Eli was one of the richest men in the world. But I found the prospect of owning even one home I'd never lived in pretty daunting. "So what's it like?" I finally asked curiously.

I was going to have to accept that Eli's life was way different from what I'd experienced, but it might take me a while to let it all sink in.

He raised a brow. "What?"

"The house next door," I said. "I've always wondered what that monstrosity looked like inside. And I can't believe you bought a vacation house just to stay in Citrus Beach for ten days."

"It will make things easier if I'm close to you," he said nonchalantly. "And the house is a good investment. Like it or not, Citrus Beach *is* growing, and the real-estate prices are picking up pretty quickly."

I leaned against the counter as I tried to figure him out. "So you bought it as an investment?"

His eyes met mine, and his intent stare made heat sizzle down my spine. "No. I bought it so I could be close to you for ten days. It's too small of a purchase for me to buy only as an investment. If I didn't have a purpose for it, I wouldn't have bothered," he answered earnestly.

Jesus! I really hate it when he says things like he just wants to be close to me.

Eli Stone was an enigma. One moment he was the quintessential aloof billionaire, and the next he was bluntly honest.

I still didn't know what to make of him and his ten-day challenge. But I swore I'd have him figured out by the time we parted ways.

I let out a nervous sigh. "I guess sometimes having money overwhelms me," I admitted. "My sister, Brooke, says I have some kind of Sudden Wealth Syndrome."

He nodded and finished off his coffee. "She's right," he answered. "I've seen it many times. Not all of my friends were born wealthy like I was, and I've seen people struggle to deal with getting rich too fast."

"Really?" I asked hopefully. "Does it go away?"

"Not always," he mused. "But you'll be fine."

"How can you be so sure?"

"Because you have me to help you get used to it, and you have a good head on your shoulders. I know it's hard when friends abandon you, and you're stuck in a whole new world. But I'll help you, Jade."

"Why?" I asked. "Why do you care?"

He shrugged. "Because I want to."

"Because you still want to sleep with me?"

He grinned. "You know I have ulterior motives, but I really do want to help."

He looked a little bit like a mischievous boy, and my heart did an enormous flip-flop.

Eli Stone was the hottest man I'd ever seen, hands down. And it was almost surreal that he was actually at my house having coffee like we'd known each other forever.

I emptied my mug as Eli stood and said, "I think our ride is here."

I put my cup in the sink and joined him at the door.

There was a helicopter overhead, and an enormous yacht that was getting close to shore, but I didn't see a car.

"Grab your clothes," he instructed as he walked outside with Charlie at his heels.

I hastily grabbed my things and locked the door, speechless as I turned around to watch the helicopter landing on the beach.

Eli held out his hand, but I hesitated.

I got the fact that we were leaving in his helicopter, now that I could see the Stone logo on the side of the aircraft. I tried to push down the panic that started to rise, the overwhelming feeling that all of this was some kind of dream, and I'd wake up very shortly.

I didn't fly in helicopters.

I didn't do impulsive things.

And I certainly didn't fly away to places yet unknown with a billionaire.

This wasn't me.

I wasn't me.

After I took a deep breath, I looked at Eli.

I shuddered as I got the sense that he was trying to tell me that my whole reality had changed, and it was time to get on with it.

"Trust me, Jade," he yelled over the sound of the helicopter.

My heart squeezed in my chest. I'd been lost for the last few months, unsure of where I was going or what the hell I was doing.

I'd been isolated and uncertain, emotions that I'd never experienced before because I *never* took a risk or stepped outside of my academic comfort zone.

But I was so damn tired of feeling misplaced and disoriented.

I needed to be me again *without* the fear and the panic. I needed to adjust or risk feeling this way for the rest of my life, and I refused to go down that road.

It's time for me to trust someone again. It's time for me to find myself, money and all.

The excitement of becoming fearless made me reach for Eli's hand.

As he pulled me toward the beach, I let my negative feelings drift away.

It was hard not to be happy when I was going to be spending my time with a very rich, hot guy, even if it was just for a little while.

CHAPTER 9

ELI

I probably should have warned Jade that we were headed out to board a megayacht that was waiting for us in deeper waters. But I had to admit that the look of surprise on her face was priceless when we landed on the upper level of the vessel. So I wasn't suffering all that much from remorse.

I reached for her hand, and when she gave it to me, I felt like somebody had slammed me in the gut.

Maybe I wanted to screw Jade more than I'd ever wanted any other woman, but I was also fascinated by her. And the fact that she was trusting me was sort of humbling.

She stumbled as she exited the helicopter, and I definitely had no problem with the fact that she fell into my arms, her body plastered against mine like we were lovers.

Hell, I wish.

"Are you kidding me?" she said as the helicopter flew away. "Is this monster yours?"

I smirked. "You don't like it?"

My intention was to let Jade get used to the things and experiences that money could buy, but having her look at me like I had two heads was rather unsettling.

"It looks like a cruise ship," she said in an awed tone.

"Not quite," I answered as I took her backpack and led her downstairs. "There are people who have bigger yachts, but it suits my needs well."

She didn't speak as we started to get under way, and seated herself by the swimming pool on the back deck.

"This is crazy," she said as she shook her head.

I flopped into the chaise next to hers as I answered, "It's San Diego. Everybody likes to get out on a boat."

One of my employees came to take our drink orders and then faded away.

Jade laughed as she continued to marvel over every single one of the yacht's over-the-top features, and I let myself relax.

There was something appealing about experiencing my world through her eyes. My motive was not to impress her, but to let her realize she now lived in the same universe that I did, and that it wasn't really all that bad.

For some reason, I felt compelled to lead her into the world of the super-rich gently. The adjustment could be good or bad, and Jade was so unspoiled that I didn't want to see her change for the worse.

I just wanted her to realize the possibilities instead of experiencing the fear that she would never really know what people wanted from her anymore.

I could introduce her to the people who were genuine.

And steer her away from the people who could do her harm.

Eventually, I wanted to see her enjoy her money, and feel comfortable spending it. Fuck knew that she'd earned that right through poverty and deprivation.

I had to give Evan Sinclair a hell of a lot of credit for including siblings he didn't know into the Sinclair legacy. The man obviously had a sense of fairness that I admired. Maybe he was protecting himself from a major lawsuit if the siblings had been discovered in the future, but from the way the billionaire had handled everything, he quite obviously gave a damn about what happened to the siblings that *weren't* born into wealth. If he didn't, he wouldn't still be so closely involved with all of them. And he definitely wouldn't have given the half-siblings a fair share. He would have paid them off for a lot less and been done with it.

I really wanted to see Jade do some kind of a fun buy to just get whatever she wanted for herself, something other than a beachfront house. The house was an investment, a roof over her head, and not really an indulgence.

To be truthful, I hadn't planned on buying the house next to hers. If I really thought about it, I felt a little bit like a stalker. But I was pretty desperate to somehow talk Jade into my bed, and I wanted that bed close by when she finally caved in.

It had been an impulse buy, but I didn't regret it.

I watched as she leaned back in her lounge chair, seemingly savoring the moment. My dick was rock-hard as I watched her face. No matter how much she protested, it was obvious that she enjoyed being on the water. Seeing her more relaxed reminded me of how much I wanted to see her after she'd had the most satisfying orgasm of her life.

"This is not *a boat*," she finally concluded as she closed her eyes. "I've been on a *boat* with my brother Aiden. He was a commercial fisherman before we all got rich. Boats are useful. This is like a floating five-star hotel. How many people does it take to run this cruise ship?"

I smiled. She was back to her usual sarcasm. "It has a full crew."

"Do you know how incredible all this seems to me?" she asked.

"Do you know how normal this is for me?" I countered. "This was actually my father's yacht. I inherited it after he died a few years ago, so I've been traveling on this *boat* for years."

"I'm sorry about your dad," she said immediately as she opened her eyes. "Is your mom still alive?"

I nodded. "She hates being on the water. She gets seasick, so she wanted me to take the yacht."

"Do you have siblings?"

I slowly shook my head. "It's just me and my mom now."

"Did you actually want this yacht?" she questioned curiously.

I shrugged. "I don't use it all that much. I have a smaller boat that I take out by myself sometimes. I prefer to be alone when I can. It's nice when I can forget who I am and just soak up the peacefulness of being on the water. But it was my dad's, and it's hard to give up something he loved."

I was spared any further comment as my employee arrived with our drinks.

After she left, Jade said, "I'm sure it's no hardship to have a yacht like this available when you want company."

I took a slug of the beer I'd ordered before I answered, "I generally don't want company. I spend most of my days and evenings surrounded by people."

"Do you ever wonder why they want to be around you?" she asked.

"I *know* why they want to be around me," I answered. "That's why I like my privacy when I have some rare free time. I know who my few real friends are, and I spend time with them when I can. But they're out of state, so we don't get to see each other all that much."

"So the public Eli Stone is different from the private one?"

"Very different," I agreed.

Most of the crazy shit I did wasn't really something I *wanted* to do. The extreme events were something I felt *driven* to do.

"So are you going to tell me that you're actually a pretty normal guy?"

"Define *normal?*" I requested.

"Do you mow your own lawn?"

"No," I answered flatly.

"Do you cook for yourself?"

"No."

"Do you ever do laundry?"

"Nope." *Christ!* In a couple of minutes, I was going to start to feel pretty useless if she didn't stop asking questions.

"Do you ever go out to the movies?"

"I have a home theater."

"Then I guess you aren't all that normal," she observed.

I hated the disappointment I heard in her tone.

"I don't do all those things because I don't have the time," I grumbled. "It wouldn't make financial sense for me to mow my lawn. I have a pretty big yard. Everything is all about managing my time."

She sat up and put her beautiful lips around the straw of her drink before she sucked up a large portion of her beverage.

I hated myself for the thoughts that entered my mind as I conjured up images of what I'd love to have those gorgeous lips of hers wrapped around right at the moment.

"I get that," she said when she finally let go of her straw. "It's not like any of my own family does their own laundry, either. Not anymore. But it's just hard to get used to. I still do everything myself."

"That's because you still aren't managing your own wealth," I told her. "Once you take over your own decisions, things get complicated, and there won't be enough hours in the day once your career as a scientist kicks in, too. There's a limit to what we can do ourselves."

"I suppose if I had been able to get a position I wanted right away, and if I managed my own wealth, I wouldn't have time for much of anything," she considered.

I frowned. "Why can't you get a position you want?"

"Not available," she said sadly. "There aren't exactly a lot of opportunities, because my focus is pretty narrow. And there's less and less money available for nonprofit positions. It's not like I didn't put in résumés just about everywhere, but there aren't many places that do genetic conservation."

"What about the San Diego Zoo?" I asked.

"I wish," she said longingly. "Getting into their genetic conservation studies would be my dream job. There's so much happening with cryogenics and genetic research. It's the future of conservation. Having the capability to do in vitro to broaden gene pools, and to bring back a decimated population, is pretty exciting."

The animation and excitement on her face as she talked about her dreams were genuine. I could see the science geek coming out, and I'd never seen anything more beautiful than watching her as her mind went to places most people's didn't.

"You could do a grant for your own research," I suggested.

"I can't do that," she answered. "I want my work to mean something, and I want somebody to think it's important enough to study and research. If I offer grants, I can't pick what they choose to do with it. Not specifically. Don't get me wrong, I'm all about giving grant money for research, and it's something I plan to do. But I don't want to insist that somebody chooses my work to research because it's my money."

My admiration for Jade shot up a couple of notches. I got what she was saying, but it took a lot of morals and ethics not to write her own ticket to success with an established research facility now that she had the money to do it.

"You've only been out of your fellowship for a few months. It will take time, but it will happen."

She smiled at me. "Don't think I've stopped trying. Since I have the time, I don't let a single possibility pass me by without applying. It will happen. It wasn't like I didn't know I'd have to work my way up, since it's a tough field."

I nodded as I stared at her determined expression. I'd always known that Jade Sinclair was an extraordinary woman. But seeing her like this, with her guard down, I was getting an even deeper insight into the person she was.

Problem was, I was beginning to like her way too much.

Control, Stone. I need to keep my emotions in check and remember that my objective is to get this woman into my bed and fuck her until my obsession with her wears off.

I did not need to get involved.

I did not need to like her.

I did not need to empathize with her.

And I sure as hell didn't need to wonder how I could make every dream Jade ever had come true.

I shrugged, a nonchalant gesture I wasn't really feeling. "You'll get there, Jade. Keep applying, and maybe try to get your wealth management under control until your opportunity comes up. Then you won't have so much to deal with all at once."

"I want to take everything over myself," she said longingly. "I'm just too afraid I'll make a mistake. I'm a scientist, Eli, not a business or money person."

"You won't screw up. And if you do, you learn from the things you do wrong. You're a smart woman, Jade. You need to give yourself credit and not be intimidated by the money. Once you settle in with it, there's so much you can do as a philanthropist. Everything changes when you realize you can help make the world a better place in some way or another. I think that's what really gets me up every single morning."

"I guess I never thought about that."

"Being privileged comes with responsibility if you're a decent person. I want to make a difference. Lots of wealthy people can and do."

She looked at me with a hopeful expression in her gorgeous eyes. "I think I'd feel better if I was doing something to help change the world. Can you help me?"

Her pleading tone almost tore the heart out of my chest, even though I'd just reminded myself of where I should be in my relationship with Jade. I was pretty sure she could ask me to jump off a cliff and fall to my death using that entreating voice, and I'd do it if I could see her happy.

I'm not exactly achieving my damn objective here.

But removing myself from Jade's emotions suddenly felt nearly impossible.

"Anything you want, Butterfly," I answered.

"I want to learn about investments. And the stock market. I want to understand how to fund-raise so I can make a difference, too. And I want to find the best conservation programs to use to donate grants for research. There are so many great projects out there, Eli. I never thought about it, but I can help other postdoc conservationists find a place to do their work."

"It will take some time," I warned her. "You're not going to learn everything in a week."

Hell, I knew I'd teach her every single thing she wanted to know. It would keep her hanging around in my life a little bit longer.

I'm not into anything long term.

Fuck! Why was I having such a difficult time remembering that?

She lifted a brow. "It's not like I'm incredibly busy, especially since you bought out my classes, even after our ten days are over."

"We'll start by going over some things every morning. And then you can come to San Diego and unofficially be my intern in my offices if you want. It's probably the fastest way to learn the most."

Damn! I hadn't planned on keeping a door open after I'd had my fill of Jade's body. But I'd just committed to much more than I'd planned.

"That would be amazing," she agreed immediately. "I'll have some survival classes, and I might get a few interviews if I'm lucky, but I'll be there every day that I'm not busy. I'd love the chance to learn from you."

Holy shit! I can think of a whole lot more personal things I'd rather teach her than business. What in the hell am I doing?

I knew I was losing control of the entire relationship between me and Jade.

None of this was part of the plan.

But somehow every detail of the temporary arrangement I'd envisioned was morphing into a different deal altogether.

I couldn't be Jade's friend.

And I sure as hell never wanted to exactly be her mentor, unless it involved both of us getting naked.

This entire ten-day bargain had been a ruse to get my dick exactly where it wanted to be. Sure, I didn't mind teaching her what I could along the way. As long as we ended up lovers, too.

I watched as she stood up and lifted the T-shirt she was wearing over her head.

Her intention to swim was obvious, but I almost groaned as she reached for the button on her jeans.

Jade had a beautiful body. She was in peak physical shape and perfectly proportioned.

Everything about the woman undressing in front of me was fucking tempting. And I felt like I was about to lose it as she kicked off her jeans and tossed them into the chair.

When she reached for her ponytail and released a mass of mesmerizing dark hair, I gritted my teeth.

"Are you coming?" she asked with what I interpreted as a come-hither smile, but probably wasn't meant to be.

My eyes devoured her. Her suit was a black, modest one-piece, but the way it clung to her body almost sent me over the edge.

"I'd like to," I grumbled to myself as I stood. And I wasn't talking about going for a swim.

She raced to the edge of the deep end and executed a perfect dive into the water.

I had to force myself to focus on getting my jeans off so I could join her.

I was relieved when I finally got into the water, wishing it was a lot colder than the lukewarm temperature that the heater maintained.

Charlie howled, and before I could stop him, he hurled himself into the pool and made a beeline for Jade. She fussed over him, crooning sweet things to the canine when he reached her.

I couldn't get mad at Charlie.

If I was a dog, I would have done exactly the same thing to get that kind of attention from Jade.

CHAPTER 10

JADE

A few days later, I realized I was actually beginning to like having Eli Stone as my neighbor.

Honestly, I was starting to like *him*, and that was going to cause an enormous problem for me.

We hit the beach for a jog every morning, and I was starting to really love having his company. I usually went alone every morning, or one of my brothers tagged along on rare occasions.

Now, Eli was there early every morning with Charlie, tossing a ball with the exuberant canine before I ever hit the sand.

As promised, Eli had spent a few hours in the morning explaining how my portfolio was put together and teaching me about the investments.

I had a whole lot to learn, but I felt better at least knowing some of the basics. He challenged me, but he was never condescending.

I guess I have a thing for hot, tattooed, hard-bodied business geniuses.

The only way I'd been able to resist his innuendos and advances was by telling myself it was just lust.

But I was quickly recognizing that I actually had a gamut of emotions when I looked at Eli, and not all of them were carnal.

Not that I didn't still think some of the things he did were over the top, but we rarely talked about his extreme hobbies. The more I got to know him, the more incongruent those actions seemed to me now.

Like he'd told me at the cabin, he seemed to be a more private type of guy, and I couldn't seem to reconcile all the crazy things I'd seen him do on television with the man I was starting to get to know.

We'd enjoyed an entire day on the yacht on day one, including an incredible meal served by a world-renowned chef from the kitchen of the enormous vessel.

Eli had finally gotten his wish when we'd sat down to an amazing meal together. It was pretty much a toss-up who enjoyed the food more. He hadn't been kidding when he'd said that he loved food, and we'd lingered a long time over that fantastic dinner.

Day two was a visit to Disneyland in a whole new way. Eli had bought out the entire park, and we rode every single ride as many times as we pleased. I'd enjoyed it because I'd only been to Disney once, and that happened solely because Noah, Seth, and Aiden had saved up the money all year, working extra shifts, to take us all as a Christmas gift. It had rained on that day, but I still remembered it as one of the best days of my younger life.

Days three and four had been a crazy trip to Las Vegas in Eli's private jet. Since I'd never been to Sin City, Eli had given me a quick introduction into all the ridiculous, extravagant things that could be done there.

By the time we'd arrived home last night, I'd been half-drunk and ready to beg Eli to take me to bed.

Fortunately, I was sober enough to remember that Eli Stone was playing a game with me, and sleeping with him was not in the plan.

Now we were on day five, but I hadn't yet discovered what Eli had planned.

Since we always went for an early-morning run on the beach with Charlie trailing behind us, it hadn't taken my brothers long to discover that I was hanging out with one of the richest men in the world.

They'd shown up at my cottage this morning, right after Eli had arrived from next door, and insisted we all go out to breakfast at the best café in Citrus Beach. Eli had agreed wholeheartedly, but I was pretty sure he'd had no idea what he'd been getting himself into when he'd taken my brothers up on a breakfast offer.

Shockingly, even my brother Noah had pushed his way into the group. It was rare when my eldest sibling took time off to go out to eat.

I watched my brothers and Eli as they all huddled together at the table in the Weston Café, talking about investments, commercial real estate, the stock market, and all of the other topics my brothers seemed to have a burning desire to learn more about.

I smiled as Eli answered every question earnestly. He'd been extremely gracious and was treating my three older brothers like they were colleagues instead of the newbie billionaires they actually were.

"It's so good to see you again, Jade," a female said as she plopped into the only vacant seat across from me. "It's been a while."

I smiled cautiously at the woman who had been my best friend for most of my life, Skye Weston. She looked good but exhausted, which wasn't unusual for Skye. She owned and managed the Weston Café, which didn't give her very many hours for things like sleep, and she burned the candle at both ends much of the time.

We'd been really close up until we graduated from high school. I'd gone off to college, and Skye had started dating Aiden. Her relationship with my brother had ended quickly and abruptly, and Skye had hastily married another man and moved to San Diego. Unfortunately, her divorce didn't happen without a lot of scandal, since her ex-husband had been convicted on several felony counts that had gotten him a life sentence.

Now, Skye was a single mom trying to deal with raising a daughter on her own.

I hadn't seen her much after her marriage and her move to San Diego. But we'd gotten together a lot since she'd inherited the café from her deceased mother and moved back to Citrus Beach with her daughter, Maya.

Skye and I had almost immediately fallen back into a best-friend type of relationship like we'd never been apart.

Then, a few weeks ago, I'd offered to help her financially so she could spend more time with Maya. She'd refused any help, and had appeared to be offended that I'd even asked.

I hadn't seen her since.

"I thought maybe you were mad at me," I finally said.

"Because you wanted to help me?" she questioned. "I wasn't *angry*, Jade. I was touched, but Maya and I have always gotten along okay. I thought maybe *you* were upset. I've called you three times and you've never called me back."

Hurt flashed in Skye's eyes, and I stopped to wonder whether her rejection had all been in my mind. Had I pushed away a good friend just because I'd felt awkward after offering her money?

I shot her a genuine smile. "I'm sorry. Things have been hectic."

She grinned back. "I can see that. I suppose dating one of the richest men in the world can be time consuming."

I quickly glanced at Eli and my brothers, noting they weren't paying a single bit of attention to our conversation. They were too busy with their own. In a lower tone, I told her, "We aren't . . . dating. We're experimenting."

"I hope by *experimenting*, you mean trying out every sexual position known to mankind. He's hot enough to melt all of the ice in the Arctic, Jade. And since he seems to hold his own quite well with your older brothers, I'm assuming he's a pretty decent guy."

"He is," I said with a sigh. "Way nicer than I expected him to be."

Skye lifted a brow. "And that's a bad thing?"

"I don't want to like him, Skye. He's not in my league."

"Don't you think that's a little judgmental?" she probed. "You're a beautiful billionaire yourself now, and even if you weren't, money doesn't make a relationship. Take my word on *that*."

I nodded. I knew Skye's ex-husband had been rich until he'd been taken down with the rest of his Italian crime family in San Diego.

"I guess it is a little irrational to think he's any different than I am. But Skye, we've seen the women he dates. How am I really supposed to believe that I'm just as gorgeous as the supermodels and celebrities he saw?"

"Maybe he's tired of skinny, superficial women. The glitter wears off pretty fast. And you're pretty, too, just not in a flashy sort of way. Give the poor guy chance. It looks like he's pursuing you if he came all the way here to see you."

"We're spending ten days together," I explained. "I think he's playing some kind of game to get me into bed with him."

Skye snorted. "Then for God's sake let him win."

I saw Aiden look in Skye's direction. His eyes stayed on her with an icy look before he finally turned his head back toward the other guys.

I'd often wondered exactly what had happened between Aiden and Skye, but it had been a whirlwind relationship that had been over soon after it had begun. And neither one of them ever talked about it. But it was weird that they completely ignored each other like they'd never met, most of the time. I had to assume the ending hadn't been all that friendly.

"I guess I don't want my heart broken," I finally admitted. "Eli is hot, but he's not the committed type. What if I end up liking him too much?"

"What if you don't try and then you always wonder if anything else could have happened between you?" she shot back. "You've never been afraid of anything, Jade. Don't start now."

"Inheriting money has changed me, Skye," I confessed. "I know most people would love to be in my position, but I feel like I'm not me anymore."

"Don't downplay how hard it is to experience a major change in your life," Skye warned. "Yes, everybody wants money until they have it, but it's kind of hard to get used to when you've always been poor, and it doesn't solve all problems. Sometimes it makes them worse."

I realized that in some ways, Skye had experienced the same things I had when she'd married a rich man. "Do you regret it?" I asked quietly.

Skye had never really talked much about her ex-husband, and I'd never met him. My few conversations with her after she'd moved to San Diego had been pretty superficial.

She nodded. "Everything except for Maya. She's my everything. If I had to do it all over again to have my girl, I would."

I smiled. "She's adorable, and a smart little cookie," I told her earnestly. "You're an amazing mom."

Skye shrugged. "I try. But I'm pretty lucky that she's such an easy kid. Let's not talk about me right now. I want to know what you're going to do with the rich hottie sitting right down the table from you."

"You're right. I guess I have to stop obsessing about what *could* happen with Eli, and just take things as they come."

I took a few minutes to tell Skye about my adventures with Eli Stone, catching her up on the last several days of crazy things we'd done.

"Oh, my God!" she exclaimed. "So not only is he mega hot, but he's thoughtful, too? Really, Jade. You have to enjoy every single moment you get with this guy."

"I know," I answered. "I'm trying to loosen up."

"That's never been an easy thing for you to do," she said gently.

I shrugged. "I'm a science geek."

"And an extremely brilliant one," Skye said. "But you're also a woman, Jade."

"Yeah, well, sometimes I have a really hard time getting in touch with that side of myself," I answered.

Until I met Eli, I hadn't ever been consumed with lust. Now, I could hardly think about anything else *except* sex.

"You still haven't done the wild thing with him? How does that happen? You're attracted to him, right?"

"Incredibly so," I told her unhappily.

"Enjoy yourself, Jade, and worry about the fallout if and when it happens," Skye advised. "He's obviously got the hots for you. He's looked over here like a million times since we've been sitting here. He wants you. You'll never know what could happen unless you let go of everything and just live in the moment."

"I've never exactly done *that*," I argued.

Skye nodded. "Your childhood was rough, but you all had each other. And you were the bravest one of the bunch. Don't wimp out now. You were the girl who wasn't afraid to go out to the middle of nowhere by herself just to commune with nature. You were the girl who would fight anybody who was a bully. And you were the type of girl who would run toward danger instead of away from it like any normal person would. You're still *that woman*, Jade. You're just confused right now. But all that will go away when you realize that you are still you, with or without the money."

Over the last few days, I'd begun to understand that everything Skye was saying now was true. Maybe I could lie back a little, learn to manage my wealth, and keep applying for the positions I wanted. My inheritance had done that for me. I didn't have to take a job I didn't want just for the income. In the meantime, I could do all I could for conservation by putting my money to work on research and projects to help rebuild dwindling populations of endangered wildlife.

The more I learned about my new wealth, the more certain I was that money was *not* going to alter my life. It wasn't going to make *me* different. But it could help me do some incredible things that I'd never imagined I'd ever be able to do in my lifetime.

I *hadn't* changed. But I did regret that I hadn't had a chance to do all of the good things I wanted to do with it now.

"You're right," I replied. "I'm starting to understand that I don't have to be terrified of my bank balance, and that I can learn to manage it. That's my main goal. Taking control of my own fortune so my half brother doesn't have that responsibility anymore. I think Evan has done more than enough for all of us."

Skye reached out and squeezed my hand. "You'll be okay, Jade. It's perfectly fine for you to just do nothing until you adjust. The money will still be there."

I felt tears spring to my eyes as I looked at Skye. She was a strong, resilient woman, and I was glad that we hadn't ended up drifting away from each other just because I was feeling confused. Skye was the type of friend who would be there no matter what. "Thank you," I said softly.

"Where exactly are you taking our sister today?" I heard my brother Noah ask as the guys all stood up.

Eli looked at all of them grimly. "It's a surprise, but I'll take care of her."

"I'm not sure I like her flying off without us knowing where she'll be," Aiden added.

I rose to my feet and got into the fray. "I'm an adult. I can take care of myself," I told my three brothers firmly.

"No offense, dude," Seth said. "But we want to know where she'll be."

"No offense taken," Eli answered smoothly. "I'll text you so it doesn't ruin the surprise."

My brothers grumbled, but seemed to accept that they weren't going to get an address.

We said our good-byes, and I promised Skye I'd call her so that she and Maya could come to my place to swim and hang out at the beach.

I felt awkward getting into Eli's expensive Bugatti Chiron. I'd teased him that I felt more like I was riding in the Batmobile than a sports car. But I got into the high-tech vehicle anyway.

"Why did you agree to text them?" I asked curiously as I fastened my seat belt.

He maneuvered the high-performance vehicle onto the street before he answered, "If you were mine, I'd want to know where you were going, too. And they're your brothers. They took care of you growing up. I can't blame them for being concerned that you're taking off with somebody they don't really know."

I rolled my eyes. "I'm almost twenty-seven years old. I have a PhD. It wouldn't be the first time that I took off by myself."

"You're not alone. You're with me. I think that's what they're worried about."

"Why?" I asked in a confused voice.

"They know I want to fuck you."

"How could they possibly know that?" I questioned.

He shrugged. "I guess it's a guy thing. We learn to read other guys so we don't step on any toes."

"And you think my brothers picked up on those male signals?"

"I know so," he said confidently.

It felt awkward to know that my brothers might know just where Eli's mind was going when he looked at me.

It felt even stranger that they might have noticed that I felt the same way.

I relaxed back into the plush seat of Eli's vehicle, wondering whether my face was as red as it felt.

CHAPTER 11

JADE

"Are you kidding me?" I squealed happily when we finally arrived at our destination. "What is all this?"

Eli looked smug as he leaned against the door of our lodgings. "We're going to be glamping here in Montana for the next four days," he informed me. "You're a genetic conservationist who hasn't really had much of a chance to do anything except *study* animal genetics and all the lab data that involves. Now you can really explore the wilderness, since I know you love doing that, too. You mentioned that you like to hike. This is probably one of the most beautiful areas to do it."

I looked around the supposed "tent" we were sharing. I raced through the large space, taking in the glamorous setup. Our luxury tent included two bedrooms, a spa-type enormous bathroom, and just about every amenity a person could find in a five-star hotel. It might have been designed to look like a tent from the outside, but the inside was full of glorious luxury.

We'd set off right after finishing breakfast with my brothers. I'd boarded Eli's jet without a clue where we were going, and I'd been kept in complete suspense until I'd gotten a chance to take in my surroundings once his jet touched down at a small airport.

On the drive here, I'd pretty much realized we were in a fairly remote area, judging by my surroundings, but it had been a toss-up for me as to exactly *where* we'd flown.

The time and direction of the plane trip had given away that we were still somewhere in the West, but it could have been one of several states.

I stopped in front of him, still stunned. "We're in Montana?"

He nodded.

Before I could think about my actions, I threw myself into his arms and squeezed him as hard as I could. "I've always wanted to come here. It's been my dream since I was a child."

My emotions swamped me as I recognized that Eli was making one of my dreams come true.

Maybe I had the funds to do my own trips now, but I would have never thought that I could stay comfortably in the middle of the wilderness. Most of my research trips were spent in a *real* tent with no running water, and bathroom facilities that were far from ideal.

His strong arms wrapped around my waist, and he held me tightly against his hard body. "If I would have known you'd be *this* happy, we would have come here on day one," he said in a teasing, hoarse voice.

I was suddenly overwhelmed with Eli's scent, a masculine, pheromone-filled aroma that completely intoxicated me. "No. I love this. And I wouldn't have wanted to miss Vegas and Disney. I'm just happy that we're here in Montana, but what exactly is *glamping*?"

"Glamorous camping," he answered, his warm breath wafting sensuously over my ear. "I jumped on board as a partner in this project with some friends, and I've actually been here a couple of times. I had a feeling you'd like it. We're in the middle of nowhere, and this area is loaded with wildlife. I was pretty sure you'd enjoy staying here. There are plenty of activities available to keep you entertained."

"How could I *not* love it?" I replied with a laugh, not the least bit surprised that Eli was one of the owners of a campground with all the luxuries. "We're camping with all the amenities. Are we really going to hike?"

"As much as you want, Butterfly," Eli answered readily. "We're not all that far from the north entrance to Yellowstone. It would have been better if we'd come during the summer so we could actually see all of the park, but we'll see what we can while we're there. The weather has been unseasonably warm."

I estimated that the temperatures were in the sixties when we'd come into the luxury tent. So it was very nice weather for Montana in the fall.

I fell into his powerful body and wrapped my arms tighter around his neck.

While it was exciting to be in Montana, being here with Eli made it really special.

It was strange, but being plastered against him felt natural, even comforting. But I had to hold back the primal urge I had to explore every inch of his body.

I pulled back to look at his face. "I hope you won't be bored."

He'd dedicated so much of his rare vacation to me, and I was grateful. But I wanted him to enjoy himself.

"Like I said, I've been here before. I wasn't able to stay long, but I thoroughly enjoyed it. We might be in the middle of nowhere, but there's plenty of entertainment if you like to fish, hike, horseback ride, and most other outdoor stuff. And the food is good."

I'd noticed that the resort was small, probably more like a boutique place for the super-rich, but I wasn't complaining. I loved to be out in the wilderness, but I personally hated not being able to take a real shower. And being exposed to the elements pretty much sucked.

It was one of the less likable parts of my job. But I'd learned to deal with it, since it put me outside so I could observe the wildlife firsthand in their natural habitat.

But I had no problem leaving the crappy part of camping out in a tent behind.

During my fieldwork, I hadn't had much of an opportunity to get outside California, so I was ecstatic about having new territory and different species to observe.

"Will you hike with me?" I asked.

"That's my plan," he answered with a smirk.

"I'm not sure I have everything I need," I said sadly. "I pretty much came with nothing."

"Although I'd very much like to see you with *nothing*, I think I've got us covered as far as hiking clothes and equipment go," he told me in a husky voice.

We stared at each other, Eli's hungry eyes devouring me. Heat shot through my body and landed squarely between my thighs.

His hand was stroking up and down my back, and his possessive expression seemed to suck out every primitive instinct I had to crawl up his body, touching and tasting every powerful muscle as I went.

"Why do you have to be so damn attractive?" I said breathlessly.

"It's our chemistry, Jade. Don't you feel it?" he said in a low growl as he took my hand and put it on his chest. "It's been there since the first time I saw you, and it's getting stronger every day. Maybe neither one of us really understands it, but I think we both *feel* it."

He reached for my ponytail and pulled my head back.

I had no desire to resist as he covered my mouth with his.

Every thought in my brain fled as Eli kissed me like I'd never been kissed before. I had no will to resist anymore, so I let everything go and opened to him. I'd *never* felt this way, and rather than be afraid of it, I wanted to savor it.

Eli made me feel like the most beautiful woman in the world, and I had no reason to think he thought otherwise. The way he consumed me was mind-blowing, and the feel of his hard body against mine was heady and exhilarating.

Needing to get closer, I wrapped one of my legs around his thighs, desperate to get relief from the almost painful ache that was violently pulsing through my entire body.

"Eli," I said breathlessly as he finally released my mouth.

"Don't think, Jade. Not now," he demanded as he grabbed my ass and pulled me up so I could wrap my legs around his hips. "Just feel how we are together."

I put my head on his shoulder as he walked us into one of the bedrooms. He dropped my body gently on the bed and came down on top of me.

Any thoughts of resisting the man who could make my body sing with pleasure had completely faded away.

I wanted Eli.

And he wanted me.

I didn't give a damn about why he was the only guy I'd ever had this kind of connection with, or what his motivations were anymore.

It didn't matter.

The only thing I needed right now was . . . him.

His eyes were like molten steel as he said, "I don't think I'm going to live another fucking day if I can't touch you."

"Then touch me," I pleaded. "Please."

I was done depriving myself and wondering what would happen in the future.

I desperately wanted Eli, and I wasn't going to be satisfied until I'd licked every inch of his gorgeous body.

Squirming beneath him with desperation, I finally wrapped my legs around his hips again.

That was when I really *felt* the truth about the way he wanted me. His rock-hard cock rubbed gloriously against my sex. There was no more alluring evidence than that. "I want this," I told him boldly as I rubbed against his erection.

"It's all yours, sweetheart," he rumbled. "I don't fucking think it works anymore for anybody else."

"Do you mean that?" I asked hesitantly as our eyes met.

"You have no idea. The only way I can even get off is to fantasize about *you*."

The delicious image of Eli stroking himself to orgasm while he thought about me danced tantalizingly through my mind.

"What were those fantasies?" I asked breathlessly. God, I'd love to make every single dirty dream this man ever had come true.

"Most of them revolved around me making you come. I want to see that, Jade. I want to watch it and I want to hear it."

"I'm not exactly vocal," I warned him as I stroked a hand down his tight jaw.

"Maybe you've just never had somebody who could make you scream," he answered arrogantly.

I pushed on his chest and sat up. "Then give it your best shot," I challenged as I pulled my T-shirt over my head.

I was so ravenous for Eli that I had no shame. I quickly unbuttoned my jeans and started to pull them off. He finished the job as he pulled them off my legs and tossed them to the floor.

I stopped and salivated as he pulled his own T-shirt off and tossed it aside. My mouth went dry as my eyes ate up every delineated muscle in his powerful chest and abs.

I landed flat on my back as Eli came back on top of me and held my wrists over my head after his greedy eyes had looked their fill at my scantily clad body.

"Jesus, Jade. You're so fucking beautiful," he rasped as he pulled the tie out of my hair and let it fan out around the pillow.

My core clenched as I felt the heat explode between our bodies. The way I needed Eli was almost terrifying, but it was also the most erotic pain I'd ever experienced. "Fuck me, Eli," I begged.

"I thought I'd never hear you say that," he growled as his mouth slammed down on mine.

I wanted to wrap my arms around him, but his hold was firm on my wrists, and the way he took control felt so damn good that I didn't care.

He never lifted his mouth from mine when he moved my wrists together and held them in one strong grip.

The clip on the front of my bra came loose with a flick of his wrist, and I moaned against his mouth as his strong hand encircled one of my breasts. He teased the hard nipple, tormenting me before he finally lifted his head.

When he moved down my trembling body, he released his grip on my wrists and cupped the mounds together until they touched.

I speared my fingers into his hair as his mouth wrapped around one of the hard tips.

"Oh, God. Eli," I moaned.

I almost came off the bed when he nipped at one pebbled nipple and then soothed it with his tongue.

Heat flowed from my core, and the knot in my stomach tightened.

I didn't know whether to pull him closer or push him away. The sensation of his hot mouth ravaging my breasts was almost more than I could take.

But I didn't stop him. I couldn't. We'd started something that *couldn't* be halted. There was no way I could handle it if Eli ceased touching me right now.

"I ache, Eli," I whimpered.

He lifted his head. "I know, baby. And I plan on taking care of that."

Eli was so confident, so intense. He seemed to know exactly what to do, while I was still confused about why my body was a mass of white heat.

I'd had one boyfriend.

And sex had never been all that exciting for me.

But Eli had upended everything I knew about pleasure, which wasn't actually very much.

I never knew that it could be this carnal, this all-consuming.

The only thing I could do was trust him, because my mind was completely fried.

He wasn't shy as he slowly licked his way down my body, tasting every inch of my flesh.

And when he finally settled his head between my legs, the first feel of that wicked tongue stroking over my panties made me come unglued.

"Eli!" I cried out as my hips rose to keep the connection between us.

Every nerve in my body fired as he pushed a finger beneath the elastic of my panties and delved into the moist heat of my pussy.

"You're so damn hot, Jade. So wet. I'm going to enjoy licking every inch of this gorgeous pussy."

I started to sweat at the thought of his wicked tongue laving over my sensitive flesh. It was something I'd never had a guy do to me before.

"You don't have to," I said hesitantly, knowing it had always been something my ex had never wanted to do.

He rose to his haunches and pulled the panties down my legs. My heart jumped as I saw the ferocious look on his face as he said, "Oh, I do *have to*, Jade. If I don't taste you right now, I'm going to lose my fucking mind. There's nowhere I want to be except between your gorgeous legs."

I watched as he spread my legs wide, then teased my slit with his thumbs, making an animalistic sound as his head dropped lower.

I closed my eyes as I prepared myself for the initial sensation of his tongue stroking over my sensitive flesh.

But there was nothing that could ever get me ready for the electric jolt that zinged through me as Eli's mouth connected with my clit.

He didn't start slow. He didn't tease. His tongue lashed boldly between my folds and consumed me like I was liquid and he had been deprived of water for way too long.

There was no way he was doing me a favor by indulging in oral sex.

He was savoring me, ruthlessly pushing me higher and higher as his tongue stroked over and over my pussy, ending every breathtaking movement with a satisfying brush over my clit.

I got lost in the furor of Eli's demanding mouth, my body a slave to every stroke of his tongue.

The knot in my belly tightened, and it kept clenching relentlessly to a point where I could barely breathe.

"Please, Eli," I pleaded. "I can't take it anymore."

I gasped as he nipped at my clit, centering all of his attention on the tiny bundle of nerves. I was helpless to do much of anything except clutch at the bedspread, hoping my grip would keep me grounded.

I screamed as the knot inside me began to unfurl, and my body shook and pulsed its way to climax. "Eli!" I screamed. "Yes."

I panted as I drifted back to Earth, Eli's face still between my legs as he wrung every drop of pleasure he could get from me.

When he finally crawled up my body, I wrapped my arms around his neck and tugged his head down to kiss him. He tasted like warm, wicked pleasure, especially since I could taste myself on his tongue.

I let him go and flopped back onto the pillow, my body completely spent.

"I thought you weren't a screamer," he said in a low voice against my ear.

"I guess I just never had a guy who made me want to scream," I said, confirming what he'd said earlier.

I smiled as he chuckled, and I let him have his moment of triumph. He'd earned it.

CHAPTER 12

Eli

Mine! Jade has always been mine!

With a possessive arm around her waist, I watched as she fell asleep with a satisfied smile on her face.

The caveman that I never knew existed inside me was rejoicing because Jade had screamed my name while she was coming, but my dick was excruciatingly hard.

My driving motivation for touching her had been alleviated. I'd wanted to see her come harder than she ever had before. It made me feel like she belonged to me, and that satisfied my primal instinct when it came to Jade. However, my body still felt like it had been dragged through pure hell.

I pushed a stray lock of hair from her face and ran a finger over her soft cheek.

Jade affected me in ways I hadn't known I could feel. I wasn't sure if that was good or bad, but I *did* know that she made me half-crazy.

Her sudden acceptance of the chemistry between the two of us had surprised me, and when she'd started taking off her clothes, it felt like every fantasy I'd ever had about her was playing out in real time.

I'd been so damn filled with lust that it had taken a while for me to recognize that she was fairly inexperienced.

Not that her lack of carnal knowledge had disappointed me. In fact, it did just the opposite. It had made me determined to show her how incredible pleasure could be, and for the most part, I thought I'd succeeded.

But I hadn't been ready for the protective instincts that had rushed up and slammed me in the gut.

There had been bliss when she'd orgasmed, but I couldn't help but notice a tiny thread of panic in her voice, too. And I fucking hated that.

I should have used a little finesse, but I lost it the minute I knew that she was going to surrender to the passion that had been raging between the two of us every single day that we were together. She'd offered herself up, and instead of using some patience, I'd gorged on her like a bloodthirsty animal.

I prided myself on my control. I always had.

I wanted Jade. But I needed her to be all in *with me.*

My inability to check myself was unnerving, but I wasn't going to let it stop me from wallowing in the sexual gratification that Jade and I could experience. Hell, I'd never felt the emotions that Jade could wring out of me, and I'd never had a woman who made me feel satisfied just by making her scream.

The possessive instincts were all new to me, and I wasn't quite sure I was comfortable with them. But if being with Jade made me into a caveman, so be it.

I *needed* her more than I *disliked* the emotions I was starting to experience.

Being careful not to wake her up, I rose from the bed, reluctant to leave her. But I needed to find my own relief. My cock was pretty pissed off that I hadn't fucked Jade, but I didn't regret it.

I could wait until Jade was completely comfortable with getting off so hard that it was scary. I was starting to like her too much to push her any harder, even if my dick was telling me to bury myself so deep inside her wet heat that I never wanted to leave.

"Shit!" I cursed as I strode toward the bathroom. "She's going to kill me."

I stripped off my jeans and boxer briefs, turned on the shower, and stepped inside.

Wrapping my hand around my cock while water pulsed against my back was becoming way too familiar to me. But if that's what it took to finally get my opportunity to be with Jade, I'd keep right on doing it.

The longer I knew her, the more I was willing to do whatever it took to be deep inside her.

I leaned against the tile, my hand running over my cock vigorously, and let my normal fantasies about Jade permeate my brain.

Mine! Mine! Mine!

In my mind, I plunged deep inside her over and over, claiming her as I watched the look of ecstasy on her beautiful face.

But my horny imaginings didn't last long enough to make me orgasm.

"Eli?"

The soft, feminine voice invaded my illusions, and I opened my eyes to see Jade's face right in front of mine.

I wasn't embarrassed because she'd caught me getting myself off. It was a normal bodily function. But I *was* shocked when she pushed my hand away and said, "I think I can do a better job."

I shuddered as I watched her drop to her knees, completely naked, and wrap her hand around my cock.

"Jade, you don't have to do that," I said with a groan.

"I do *have* to," she argued. "I *need* to."

I leaned back on the tile and closed my eyes when she wrapped her sensual lips around my dick. For a moment, I wasn't completely sure that I hadn't conjured her up in my fantasies, but when she sucked hard, I knew damn well it was real. My fantasies had never been this good.

It occurred to me that she'd done this sexual act before, but had obviously never gotten it reciprocated by her prick of an ex-boyfriend. *The bastard. He has no idea what he missed.*

A throaty groan left my mouth as she gingerly played with my balls while she was trying to swallow my cock.

"Jade. You're fucking killing me," I rasped. Grabbing her hair, I gently guided her to the rhythm I desperately needed. I figured if I was going to die, there was no better way to go.

She adjusted immediately, and my heart started to hammer hard enough that I wondered if she could hear it.

The driving need to watch her made my eyes fly open, and I looked down to see Jade, her eyes closed, and a look of complete gratification on her gorgeous face.

"Fuck!" I tore my eyes from her. Shit was getting too intense, and I couldn't watch her without making myself insane.

I felt her wrap her fist around the back of my shaft, a tight friction that made me put my hand behind her head and urge her to go faster.

My impending orgasm was building fast, and I knew I was going to come hard. "I'm going to come, sweetheart," I warned her, giving her enough time to retreat.

She literally purred, and the vibration set me off.

Every muscle in my body tensed, and my head fell back against the wall as I exploded. I groaned, feeling like I was never going to stop coming, as Jade swallowed every single drop.

"Holy hell!" I yelled in a voice I didn't quite recognize as my own.

Jade had completely destroyed me.

But it had felt so damn good that I didn't care.

I pulled her to her feet and pinned her against the tile. "Why in the hell did you do that?" I asked desperately, my mind still scrambled.

She smiled at me, a sultry curve of her lips that I'd never seen before. "Because I wanted to," she answered. "What you did to me, how you made me feel . . . it was amazing, Eli. I wanted to see if I could do the same thing to you."

"Did I scare you?" I asked huskily, my voice hinting at remorse.

She shook her head. "Not you. I was just a little afraid of how my body reacted. But it was worth it."

I leaned down and kissed her, savoring the taste of myself on her lips.

Mine! Mine! Mine!

I ignored the caveman chant and pulled her wet body into mine. I wrapped my arms around her possessively before I said, "Mission accomplished, sweetheart."

"You didn't fuck me," she said sadly against my shoulder.

If I wasn't completely limp for the first time since I'd met her, I would have given her exactly what she wanted.

"I will," I warned her. "But I'm a guy who understands the importance of foreplay."

She laughed, and it was a carefree, happy sound that made my damn chest ache.

Jade pulled back and looked at my face, her hand stroking over my jaw as she answered, "Then I think I'm a very lucky woman."

I grinned back at her. "I'm not exactly complaining, either."

Hell, the soft, curvy woman who was naked in my arms had just rocked my entire world.

And I was pretty damn happy about it at the moment.

Screw my control!

Nothing else mattered but her as I slammed the shower off, picked up the female who had turned my life upside down, and carried her to bed.

CHAPTER 13

Jade

When I woke up early the next morning, I finally realized exactly what Eli had meant when he'd said that he *had us both covered*.

When I opened the suitcases that were just inside the door, I found an enormous amount of hiking gear, jeans, sweatshirts, jackets, and anything else I could ever need to face the Montana wilderness in the beginning of October.

I'd taken my time to poke around the two-bedroom tent, which was honestly more like a luxury cabin, marveling over some of the furniture that had obviously been hand carved. It was beautifully done, but it still gave the place a rustic feel.

When I'd discovered a brochure, I was surprised by just how many activities were offered. We were obviously close to some kind of civilization if they had white-water rafting, horseback riding, fishing, and a multitude of other outdoor offerings.

I'd found Charlie, who must have arrived later last night, lying on a fluffy rug near the door. He'd been asleep while I'd been surfing through the clothing, but he was wide awake as soon as he heard my voice.

"Hey, buddy," I crooned to the canine as he rose and came to me, his tail wagging happily as he accepted the affection like it was his right to get it. "Did you get shut out of the bedroom? I wondered why you didn't come with us."

"He had a spa appointment," Eli said from the bedroom door. "He really loves to go there, so my jet brought him here after he was done."

I looked at Eli to see if he was joking, but I saw no evidence that he wasn't telling me the truth.

I lifted an eyebrow. "A *spa* appointment?"

Eli shrugged. "Charlie was in pretty bad shape when he came into the animal shelter. He'd suffered a lot of abuse. He didn't really like people very much, but he loved to go to grooming. I think it has something to do with the treats he gets. But he seemed to like the people, too."

All right, dammit. The way that Eli cared about his previously maltreated dog really *did* get to me. How many billionaires made the time to care this much about a pet?

"Good morning," he said as he came over and gave me a kiss.

I stopped fussing over Charlie and wrapped my arms around Eli's neck. "Good morning to you, too."

I had wondered whether things would be awkward with him today, but they weren't. It was kind of like we'd broken through some of the tension between us. So everything felt pretty natural.

I savored his masculine scent as he held me close, a possessive arm around my waist.

Last night had been an amazing experience for me, and I didn't regret shoving my reservations aside one bit.

Maybe I was still a little scared, but I could live with some trepidation if last night was my reward for overcoming it.

Finally, I stepped back. "Coffee," I said. "Must have coffee. I won't be fully functional until I do."

He shot me a wicked grin before he let me go. "Does that mean I can take advantage of your befuddled state?"

"No," I said with a laugh. "Oh, no you don't. I'm thoroughly addicted to caffeine. I'm single-minded until I've had at least two cups."

"I bet I could change that," he grumbled as he started to set up the coffeemaker.

I bet you could, too.

I had to force myself to stop looking at his godlike body that was only wrapped in a towel, probably the one he'd dropped when he'd taken us both to bed.

It would be so easy to strip Eli of his towel and beg him to fuck me. But things were so good between us right now that I wanted to savor the emotions. There was no way I wanted this to end. Not yet.

I'd pulled on the smaller robe in the bedroom closet. I was completely covered, so I didn't mind getting down on the floor to cuddle Charlie. I hated the thought that anybody had even tried to break his intrepid spirit.

Charlie took love and gave it back. I wished the whole world could be as straightforward as Eli's dog.

"You smell good," I told Charlie as I scratched his belly, which caused him to wriggle his solid body like there was no greater pleasure in his world.

"That's one perk of letting him finish his grooming before he got here," Eli said as he handed me down my coffee. "He doesn't stink."

One Splenda and lots of cream!

I knew he'd gotten it right the moment I took my first sip.

Eli Stone was definitely a detail guy.

I'd always wondered if he'd had his assistant arrange our outings, but I was beginning to think that he played a significant role in planning everything.

"You're pretty lucky," Eli observed as he sat down half-naked on the sofa with his coffee. "There are very few people that Charlie really likes."

"I guess I have a way with animals," I told him as I stood up. "They know I love them, so they usually love me back. And I feel honored that Charlie gives me love. It's really hard for any creature that has been abused to trust a human again. Really, animals are amazing that way."

"Yet you don't have a pet of your own," Eli commented.

"I had a hamster when I was a kid," I said with mock defensiveness. "And we couldn't afford to feed a dog. My brothers were working too hard just to keep us together. But I've been thinking about getting a dog. I'm just not sure where I'll end up working. If I take a job in the field, I could end up somewhere a dog doesn't really want to be, like a sweltering hot jungle. So I'm waiting to see what happens first."

"I don't think you should be anywhere dangerous," he rumbled.

"Now you sound like one of my brothers," I teased.

"I like your brothers."

"I love them," I admitted. "But they can be a little too protective sometimes."

"I noticed," he answered. "They grilled me pretty thoroughly in the café."

"I guess I was too busy talking to Skye to notice anything except their inquisition at the end. I'm sorry. They've made invading my privacy into an art form."

"I don't mind," he remarked. "I could tell that their questions were coming from a good place. They love you, too. They don't want to see you get hurt."

"But I'd really like them to see that I'm all grown up. It's not that I don't need them anymore, but it would be nice if they could see me as a responsible adult."

"That's never going to happen, Butterfly. You didn't grow up together. They raised you, and I'm willing to bet that they feel more of a parental responsibility toward you." He handed me another small brochure. "Check this out and let me know what's on the agenda for today."

I took the small booklet from his hand and started looking carefully over the multitude of activities offered. Unlike the general brochure, this booklet had dates and times.

"I have no idea what you'd like to do," I muttered as I looked over the large list of things to do while residing in the world's biggest "tent" that was climate controlled and offered every available luxury. "I'd love to go horseback riding."

"I can ride," he answered.

I looked up and met his eyes. "I'm not very good. I traveled by horse a few times to complete some wildlife studies. But this would probably be a lot better."

"We can go today," he answered. "Do you want to hike tomorrow?"

"You know I do," I said enthusiastically.

"This trip is for you, Jade. It's not about me. Pick whatever you like."

My heart ached from his words.

I was his priority.

And all he wanted was for me to have a good time.

While I thought he was being sweet, I didn't want to decide alone and leave him stuck doing things he wouldn't like.

"But I want *you* to have fun, too. You never get time to take a vacation, Eli. This has to be about you, too."

"Like I said, I've been here before. A couple of times, actually, so I've done a lot of those things," he informed me, nodding his head toward the brochure.

I picked out a few activities from the list, and we planned the next couple of days together before we ordered breakfast in our luxury tent.

When we'd finished eating, I rummaged through the suitcases.

"How did you know what size I wore?" I asked curiously as I took out a pair of jeans that were my exact size from the suitcase, and then removed a sweatshirt.

I stopped as I saw all of the matching lingerie sets.

I noticed that they, too, were my size.

"I might have looked in your bedroom while you were in the kitchen at your house," he confessed, not sounding the least bit sorry.

"If you were poking into my underwear to keep this a surprise, you probably noticed I'm not really all that into nice lingerie."

"I know," he rumbled. "But I wasn't about to buy you anything a billionaire wouldn't wear. I'd look like a cheap bastard."

I sighed as I picked up a black bra with matching panties. They were lacy, silken, and beautiful. "I guess they'll have to do," I teased as I added them to my pile and picked everything up.

"Look in the zippered area of the big suitcase," he said. "I brought you back something that belongs to you."

As he requested, I felt around in the pocket once I'd gotten it open.

To my surprise, I pulled out the book I'd been reading the day Eli had arrived in the backcountry, and a work of science fiction.

"I've been wondering where that went," I told him as I examined the steamy romance paperback.

"I didn't take it intentionally," he said in a remorseful voice. "I know how it is when you've started a book and want to read the rest. I picked up both books while I was packing up, but had yours sticking out of the top so I could hand it over to you. I guess I got distracted."

"Is this one good?" I asked as I put the sci-fi book on the coffee table.

"So far," he replied. "I haven't gotten very far into it yet."

I went to lay my book beside his, but then thought better of it and put it on top of my pile of clothing.

"Toss it there," he suggested. "Maybe we can get in some time to read."

Eli had obviously seen my reluctance, and my face started to turn pink.

"It's dirty," I told him.

"Looks like a romance," he said nonchalantly.

"It is. An incredibly steamy one."

"How's the story?"

"Really good. She's one of my favorite authors."

"Then why did you hesitate to put it down?"

"Because it really is dirty," I explained.

"It's a book that you want to read. I read sci-fi to escape. I think most people read to take a break from the real world," he answered. "Besides, I like it when you're dirty," he said in a dangerously sexy voice.

I dropped the book next to his sci-fi title. Eli obviously didn't give a damn if I read erotic romance. I wasn't sure why that fact touched me so much, but it did.

"Thanks," I said.

"For what?"

I could thank Eli for a lot of things.

Thanks for caring about my sexual pleasure.

Thanks for caring about your dog so much.

Thanks for the incredible experiences I've had over the last week.

Thanks for noticing the small things, because it makes me feel important.

Thanks for every single day I've spent in your company, because you're so much fun to be with, and so damn considerate and nonjudgmental.

In the end, I settled with "Thanks for being you."

I walked out of the room and headed toward the bathroom so I could take a shower.

CHAPTER 14

ELI

I spent the next few days trying to figure out what was even remotely good about *me* being *me*, but I couldn't think of one damn thing to justify Jade's gratitude.

Mostly, I was a workaholic. My break with Jade was the longest I'd ever taken since my dad had passed away.

I didn't do commitments, so I had no fucking idea how to be good to a girlfriend. But the idea of claiming Jade in some way was starting to look pretty damn appealing.

And maybe Charlie was a little spoiled, but it wasn't difficult to spend my free time with him, and he deserved an owner who treated him well. He'd spent way too much of his short canine life in misery.

Honestly, I thought Jade deserved better than a guy who was only around so he could satisfy his carnal urges.

I was thoroughly convinced that once we'd gorged ourselves on sex, one of us would eventually get bored and move on.

Problem was, I wasn't so sure I'd be the one who wanted to break things off quickly once our itch was scratched.

So I'd avoided having sex with Jade, even though it was fucking killing me.

The longer it takes for us to have sex, the longer she'll be around, right?

I'd made certain we were worn out every single day with planned activities: exploring Yellowstone, bike riding, horseback rides, white-water rafting, and some very long hikes.

By the time our day was over and we'd had a few drinks after dinner, Jade had conked out almost as soon as she hit the bed.

I wasn't quite so lucky.

There was no way I was going to sleep in another bed. I liked feeling her warmth draped over me, or snuggled up to my side.

But every night was torture.

I couldn't figure out what in the hell was wrong with me. I'd achieved my goal. Jade was willing, and we were both adults. Why the fuck was I putting off what I knew would be the most satisfying sex of my entire life?

She's making me crazy.

There was no other explanation.

Our days had been an eye opener for me. Although I'd already known that Jade was gutsy, because of her survival expertise, I'd also discovered just how fearless she was when confronted with *any* kind of outdoor activity.

She jumped into every experience wholeheartedly and without any hesitation.

I wasn't quite sure if that fascinated me even more, or if it terrified the hell out of me.

"Do you think we should head back?" Jade asked, jolting me out of my own thoughts.

I looked around, realizing we could either take the trail back to our camp, or we could hike farther away from our lodgings before circling back.

The moment I looked at Jade, my dick was hard. Not that it wasn't constantly that way because of her, but it was difficult not to want to fuck her up against a nearby tree.

Her skin was still flushed with excitement, even after exploring for two days. And her joyous smile made me feel like somebody had bashed me in the chest.

Her happiness was becoming my damn obsession just because I wanted to keep looking at her smile.

We'd gotten lucky for the last few days. The weather had been good, but cold, so we were both bundled up for hiking.

I looked at the sun, and then my watch. "We probably should head back. I don't want to get caught in the woods after dark."

It was rutting season for the big-horned-mammal population like elk and moose, and I'd been ridiculously paranoid about Jade stepping on a rattlesnake since the minute we'd first started hiking. We'd seen plenty of the former, but hadn't seen *any* kind of snake while we'd been out hiking. But it didn't lessen my fear of it happening to her.

I turned to lead the way back to our luxury lodgings, but turned back around as I heard Charlie growling, a serious sound I'd never heard from him before.

"Don't move," Jade said in a calm voice. "And don't run."

I looked up the opposite trail just in time to see a huge grizzly bear rear up onto its hind legs.

I had to force myself to keep my hands at my side and not jump for Jade to get her out of harm's way.

That bear would have to tear my ornery ass up before it ever got to Jade.

"Bear spray?" I asked in a quiet, monotone voice.

"Not close enough," she answered. "And probably not necessary. He's prehibernation, and is probably just looking for food of the non-human variety."

As she spoke, I did see Jade slowly reach for her bear spray just in case. Since I wasn't exactly a country boy, I'd let her talk me out of carrying it myself. I'd relented since she had way more experience with wildlife than I did. But I had never stopped to think about the possibility that she could be torn up if the weapon didn't stop a bear.

The male was still on his hind legs, and it wasn't sitting well with me that Jade was several steps closer to the bear than I was.

The beast was probably fifty feet from us, and not making any crazy moves that made me twitchy. Still, it was *too damn close*.

"Don't make eye contact," she instructed. "And no sudden moves."

I hastily moved my eyes from the massive animal's face, and motioned for Charlie to be quiet and get down beside me. I was relieved when he reluctantly obeyed.

I stayed frozen in place while Jade was talking nonsense in a calm voice to the bear.

Strangely, her vocal calmness appeared to be working.

"Start backing up slowly," she instructed in the same tranquil tone she was using with the bear. "Let's give him some space."

I waited until Jade was beside me before I started my retreat.

If something was going to happen with the massive mammal, I was damn well going to be able to put my body between hers and the bear's to keep her from getting mauled.

"When do we haul ass and get out of here?" I asked in a quiet voice as I motioned for Charlie to follow us.

"We don't," she said firmly as we kept giving the predator more and more space. "If we act like prey, his instinct is going to make him pursue. And a human will never be able to outrun a grizzly."

With every step we took, the more distance we put between us and the bear. "Do we just keep moving like this?" I asked.

"Yes. You're doing fine. We can't turn our back on a bear until he can't see us. Bad idea. Just keep walking until he moves on."

Once I'd gotten over my immediate instinct to protect Jade by throwing her body to the ground and covering her—a move that would have probably gotten us both mauled—I respected her judgment. She *was* the expert. When we'd come across rutting moose and elk, she'd steered me away from them carefully, teaching me how to keep from getting hurt.

"He's leaving," she remarked.

I looked up to see the bear turn his back on us and lumber in the other direction. Obviously, it didn't matter if the *bear* turned his back on *us* since it was an apex predator.

As the grizzly finally disappeared into the woods, Jade said, "We can move on."

I grabbed her hand in an iron grip as she turned around and kept up a fairly fast walking pace toward our accommodations.

"Are you still concerned?" I asked her after we'd moved at a steady clip for a few moments, nodding my head at the bear spray she was still holding in her hand.

"No," she answered in a normal voice. "He looks well fed, and I didn't see any sign that he's likely to be aggressive and stalk us. But bears can be unpredictable. No harm in being prepared."

I sure as hell didn't like the sound of *that*. "I've been here before, and I've hiked. I've never seen *any* bear, much less a grizzly. We take precautions. Usually, we only allow hiking in groups of three or more, and with an experienced guide. And in the three years the place has been operational, not a single guest or employee has seen a grizzly. Not this far away from the park."

"Their numbers are recovering," she informed me. "They've been protected to increase the population, and now they're starting to spread out beyond the Yellowstone ecosystem. That's been happening for a while now. But I don't think they're here very often. I didn't see the usual signs. It was probably just an uncommon occurrence."

I frowned. "Do you think it will cause any problems at the resort? Are the guests in danger?"

She shook her head. "No more than somebody staying in the park. A person has a better chance of getting struck by lightning than getting attacked by a bear. The large percentage of attacks are due to human error. I'm not saying it doesn't happen without provocation, but it's extremely rare."

"Human error? Like running?"

"Sometimes. One of the biggest mistakes is getting too close to cubs. Females are incredibly protective."

"You don't sound the least bit nervous about coming face to face with a grizzly," I grumbled.

"I'm not," she told me. "I'm excited. That wasn't my first bear encounter, but it's my first grizzly. Don't get me wrong, we didn't need to be that close. And I respect the fact that the bears are wild animals, and anything could happen. But I've always wanted to see one in their natural environment."

Fuck! She was actually flushed with excitement and smiling.

"This has happened to you before?" I asked.

"Of course. I did all kinds of fieldwork, Eli. I'm a wildlife conservationist. Granted, I never got outside California, but we have plenty of bears."

"I don't like it," I answered stubbornly. "It's a dangerous job."

She moved closer and slammed into my shoulder playfully. "Most of the time, I study data in a laboratory. Running into a bear is a rarity."

"They can be aggressive." *Jesus!* Didn't she know that something bad could have happened?

"He was up and sniffing. That's usually curiosity and not aggression. But I agree. He was a huge male. But *we* were invading *his* territory. That's always a very small risk that you take when you hike. Especially in this area."

"I was more worried about snakes," I said, pissed off at myself because I'd hardly considered other risks.

"Human-and-bear encounters happen. But being mauled or killed by one is a rarity. For the most part, they'd rather avoid humans."

"No more hiking," I told her as we arrived at our tent.

I waited until she was inside, and then closed the door behind us. It was going to take a hell of a long time to forget the sight of her in front of me while we were having a confrontation with a damn grizzly.

Maybe *she* was able to handle it well, but I was probably going to have nightmares about what could have gone wrong.

I bent down to reassure my canine, who was clearly still confused by what had happened. "Good boy," I told him as I stroked his head.

Charlie was easy. After a minute of affection, he was back to normal.

Jade took off her jacket and bent down to pet Charlie, too. "He *was* a good boy. If he wasn't so well trained, we could have had trouble on our hands."

As I straightened up, I asked, "So what do you do if a bear charges?"

She took off the belt around her waist, and dropped the hiking tools and bear spray on the kitchen counter.

"It depends," she replied. "Sometimes they'll do a fake charge to get you to move away. But if they're really going to engage, you wait until they're within twenty-five feet or closer and hit them with bear spray." She looked up at me and added, "Hey, you really look worried. Are you okay?"

"Not completely," I admitted. "I was afraid you'd get hurt."

"You were worried about me?" she questioned softly, her expression slightly surprised.

"For God's sake, I brought you here, Jade. And something could have happened to you because I picked the wrong damn place to go."

I wasn't afraid to admit I'd been pretty damn scared that the bear would go rogue and hurt her.

And it would have been my fault.

"I'm fine, Eli. I *was* nervous the first time I had a close encounter with a bear. But I guess I've learned that the worst thing a person can do is panic. I've had years of experience and research into animal behavior. You haven't. I know it's pretty terrifying."

"I wasn't afraid for me," I rasped. "I was worried that something would happen to you. One mistake and you could have been dinner."

She came forward and touched my arm. "We didn't make a mistake, Eli."

I had her in my arms before she could blink, and I held her so tightly she probably couldn't breathe.

We stayed that way for a couple of minutes, and the feeling of her safe body against me eventually calmed my ass down.

"Are you okay?" she asked.

I released her slowly. "Yeah. I'm good."

I was a damn liar. I still didn't really want to let her out of my sight.

Lighten up, Stone! If she wasn't scared before, I'm probably making her anxious with my behavior.

"I should make a few calls and let the local wildlife stations know that we had a grizzly encounter. They like to monitor when the bears begin moving away from the park."

I took off my jacket and started to remove my boots. "No problem. We can go to dinner right after that."

"Thanks for caring about my welfare," she said softly.

I looked up at her from my stooped position. "Thanks for making sure we weren't on the dinner menu for Smokey."

She laughed as she rummaged for her cell phone.

I kicked off my boots, determined that I'd never see Jade in danger again.

My damn heart would never survive if I had to see her vulnerable and not be able to do anything about it a second time.

CHAPTER 15

JADE

Our last day at the mountain resort was bittersweet for me. I wished we could stay longer, but Eli had been true to his word, and we weren't hiking at all today. Instead, he'd made me pick out an activity that would involve more people in one spot.

I knew he'd been scared about the bear encounter, and I also realized that he'd been terrified for my safety.

For some reason, his worry had touched me more than it really should have, considering we *had* been facing an enormous grizzly. But I had sensed his fear, and I could feel that he wasn't worried about himself getting mauled.

His concern had all been for me, so I wasn't about to complain about not hiking.

I'd chosen a beginner class to learn how to rappel down a rock face.

I'd done some easy free climbing, more out of necessity to view wildlife than as a hobby. As I glanced up at the rappel spot, I realized why Eli had chosen to sit this one out. I estimated the height to be no more than forty feet, and Eli was an experienced aided climber who had taken on some of the toughest rock faces in the world.

The relative ease of the task didn't dampen my enthusiasm. I was elated to start learning to climb, and rappelling was a skill I needed to have if I was going to take on some bigger cliffs.

I looked over at Eli as he spoke with the instructor. They appeared to be deep in conversation, and I had to wonder again why he wasn't very thrilled about this particular class.

Is it because he's already an expert climber? Or is there something else bothering him?

He'd been reserved since we'd had our bear encounter yesterday, and he seemed even more distracted this morning.

Maybe he's just anxious to get back to work.

I had no doubt that he'd fallen behind because of the time we'd spent together, but I was determined to be there to help him catch up when we returned to San Diego. I was learning so much during our morning sessions, and I was convinced I could keep learning while I was acting as Eli's unofficial intern. My hope was that I could take the load off him just a little once I got up to speed on his businesses.

I looked at my classmates for the rappel. There were three others who were standing around finishing their morning coffee, and I smiled as two of them looked up and waved at me before resuming their conversation.

I zipped up my coat after I'd tossed my empty coffee cup into the trash. It was still early, and it was kind of frigid. The temperatures were starting to get colder, especially during the night. Not that I really noticed until I got outside. The lodgings were warm and toasty, and came complete with a wood-burning fireplace.

I put my hands in my pockets to warm them up as I glanced again at Eli and the instructor. They were still having a conversation, and neither one of them looked all that happy.

Eli had made some phone calls last night after I'd called the local wildlife biologists who kept track of the bears in the area. I didn't remember him getting into bed because I'd drifted off before he'd even gotten to the bedroom.

But I did recall waking up sprawled on top of him. I was pretty sure my body was like a heat-seeking missile when it came to Eli. If he was close, I'd find him.

The biologist I'd talked to had pretty much confirmed that seeing a grizzly near our location was unusual, and they caught me up on what was happening with the bear population. Although the sighting was an isolated incident, the grizzlies were starting to get farther and farther away from the park. So biologists and conservationists had their work cut out for them with the local ranchers and farmers to prevent the conflict that would inevitably happen.

I let out a sigh. I didn't envy the people working on the issue. While they were rejoicing about the possibility of the Yellowstone grizzlies possibly meeting with the Glacier National Park grizzlies someday to ensure better genetics, the fallout from the big bears expanding their territory was daunting.

I walked around the rock face and discovered a makeshift set of stairs behind the incline, obviously an easy way up for new climbers. My classmates were slowly making their way up the steps, but I scrambled up the rocks, needing some activity to keep my blood circulating.

Once on top, I viewed the area. I could see the cabins and so-called *tents*. We hadn't wandered very far from the resort, a fact that I was certain Eli had planned.

There were maybe twenty dwellings, each one extravagantly furnished, I was certain. It was definitely a boutique-type place, a location that catered to people who could afford to vacation in the wilderness but retain all the conveniences of the city.

I'd nearly gagged when Eli had told me the price to rent one of his glam tents, and I'd been even more surprised when he shared that they were pretty much booked up year-round with an enormous waiting list.

The lodging we were using was generally kept open for the partners. When they knew nobody was going to be using it for a while, they'd rent it out for an enormous price.

Honestly, I was beginning to think that the resort was a pretty savvy investment. If it was so exclusive that Eli had a huge waiting list, it made people even more willing to drop a fortune for some relaxing time in the woods. Granted, the only people who could really afford to come here had some pretty deep pockets, but there were plenty of wealthy people across the country.

"Are you experienced?" a curious voice asked from behind me.

I turned to see a middle-aged woman who looked terrified.

I smiled at her, hoping to reassure her. "I've never rappelled, but I've hiked and climbed up plenty of mountains in California."

"Are you scared?" she asked.

I shook my head. "No. And you don't need to be, either. I'm sure our instructor will make sure we're all safe."

I didn't want to dismiss her trepidation. Maybe I wasn't afraid, but everyone had different fears. For me, it was just a bunch of boulders stacked on top of each other, but it might look like a scary cliff to her.

"I'm afraid of heights, but my husband thinks it's silly to worry," she said, verifying my suspicion that being on top of *anything* made the woman wary.

"Nobody is going to force you to go," I said gently.

"My husband will never let me hear the end of it if I don't. We're trying to start pushing our boundaries. I might be afraid, but I guess I'll do okay."

"If you *want* to do it, you'll be great," I told her.

She patted my forearm and said, "Thanks, honey. You be careful going down," she warned before she took a few steps back into the group that I assumed contained her unsympathetic husband. By the apparently easy conversation that was going on, I was guessing the other young man was her son.

I decided to go see what was holding Eli and the instructor up when I spied an enormous bird flying over my head. Distracted, I watched it land on a tree at the edge of the woods.

Shading my eyes, I stepped forward to get a closer look, noting that I was close to the edge of the drop. Keeping my feet steady, I reached into my pocket for my camera. With the zoom, I was pretty sure I could get a decent picture.

"Jade! Get away from that fucking edge now!"

I was so focused on getting a photo that Eli's extremely loud bellow from beneath me startled me. It wasn't a casual warning. He'd sounded like he was terrified, his voice booming out across the resort.

My foot went a little bit forward as my body startled, and before I could completely correct my balance, I felt myself tilting over the edge.

I flapped my arms like I was the bird I was just watching, but inevitably lost the fight to regain my balance.

I was no bird.

And I was totally unprepared for the fall.

The first thing I felt was the pain from my body hitting the unforgiving rock.

Then there was Eli's hoarse cry as I hit the hard ground.

After that, there was only darkness.

CHAPTER 16

Eli

"You really need to eat, Eli," I heard my mother's voice say in a gentle tone.

My vision was blurred from lack of sleep, but I wasn't hungry at all.

The last two and a half days had been like a nightmare that I'd experienced while I was completely awake. And I still didn't feel like I'd been able to step out of my bad dream.

If I lived to be a century old, I knew I'd never forget the sight of Jade lying broken and bleeding at the bottom of the rappel cliff.

I was guessing my fear over the bear had just been a prelude to what was about to come.

And I thought we were doing something relatively safe.

We'd gotten Jade to a small local hospital after her fall, and they'd almost immediately transferred her by air to Billings, where she'd been stabilized. They'd fixed her dislocated shoulder, popping it back into place without major surgery, and she was going to recover from her skull fracture.

Her physician had allowed her to be transferred back to San Diego by air earlier in the day, but she was still in intensive care.

She had woken up several times, but was allowed to sleep again as soon as the medical staff determined that she was as oriented as she could be with pain medication on board.

"Thanks, Mom, but I'm not hungry," I muttered, keeping Jade's smaller hand clutched in mine.

I felt a hand clap on my shoulder. "Dude, you need to take a break. We're all here now. We got this. Go eat and get some sleep."

I looked up to match the voice with the face. For the most part, Jade's brothers all sounded alike.

It was Noah, and he had a determined look on his face.

"I'm good," I protested.

"She's not going to die while you go take care of yourself," he rumbled. "And you're not doing her any good by getting this sleep deprived."

"I'll sit by her side while you're gone," a soft, feminine voice said from my other side.

I glanced up at Jade's twin, Brooke, as she nudged me to move off the chair.

Standing up reluctantly, I watched as Jade's sister took my place. "Go," she instructed. "Jade wouldn't want you to wear yourself out like this, Eli. You were with her for over two days when she needed you. Let us help now."

There were several bodies present around the room. Since Jade wasn't considered critical, they allowed all of us to hang out in the private room.

Everyone there was related to Jade, except for Brooke's husband, my mother, and me.

My mother had shown up after I talked to her on the phone to explain that I wasn't going to be able to host the fund-raiser that I'd promised for Jade's charity. Mom had taken over and postponed the event, calling every attendee and vendor to reschedule with the help of my assistants.

"I'll be back," I said firmly.

"Is that a threat or a promise?" Aiden said jokingly. "She'll be fine, Eli. My brothers and I have taken care of her most of her life. It's not like we haven't seen her sick or banged up before."

Maybe *they* had seen her hurt, but I hadn't, and her condition had kept me glued to her hospital bed nonstop for a few days.

I'd been there with her in Billings when she was making anguished cries of pain while they were putting her shoulder back in place.

Jesus Christ! If I never heard her hurting and in pain again, it would be too soon. Her agony had ripped my heart out, leaving a clawed wound in my chest that I wasn't sure would ever heal.

"Call me if she wants anything," I conceded as I stepped up close to my mother.

"I think she's pretty much out cold for now," Seth commented. "It's probably better that way. It will give her body a chance to heal."

My eyes flew back to Jade, examining every scrape, laceration, and bruise on her visible skin.

"We got lucky," I grumbled.

She'd landed on her left side, dislocating her shoulder and glancing her head off a nearby rock. But her initial body landing had broken her fall, and her head didn't take a direct hit. If things had happened even slightly different, she could have had a much worse head injury.

"We all know it could have been even more serious," Noah said somberly. "But it's best not to dwell on that. If you do, it drives you crazy. Take it from me . . . I've been in the hospital with all of my younger siblings more times than I can count. Every one of those incidents scared the shit out of me. But they all got through it."

Even though I knew that Noah was just a few years older than I was, his presence seemed to be a stabilizing factor for everybody.

When Brooke had arrived from the East Coast in hysterics, Noah had calmed her down with his steady demeanor.

He'd talked to all of Jade's half-siblings and cousins on the phone, using the same even, stable tone and logical thinking to convince them that Jade was okay, and that they didn't need to come to California to be with her.

Owen was also reassured that he didn't need to interrupt his busy residency schedule to make his way back to California, since Jade was stable.

It was like Noah just *knew* how to calm everybody at the same time, probably a skill he'd acquired while he was caring for his younger siblings.

He must have felt like he had the weight of the world on his shoulders.

"I had your assistant bring dinner for everybody," my mom said as she put her hand on my arm. "Let's go eat."

"If you don't go, I'm going to go back to the dining room and inhale your food," Seth joked. "It was really good."

Everybody else murmured their agreement. Apparently, the only one who hadn't eaten was me.

I quietly followed my mother out of the room, to an empty dining area right outside the room that the staff had set up for the family.

Since it wasn't common procedure to accommodate visitors this way in the ICU, I was pretty sure that my mother had insisted since she and I were both very large donors to the research facilities.

"Sit down before you fall down," my mother ordered.

I complied, since I'd heard that tone of voice my whole life, and I knew better than to argue with it.

"I'm fine," I lied. "I'm just tired."

My mother fussed with making me a plate, slapping it down in front of me within a few minutes. "Don't lie to me, Elias," she warned. "I always know when you aren't telling me the truth."

Jesus! I fucking hated it when she used my full name. She was the only woman who could make me feel like a contrite kid when I was a well-respected, and sometimes feared, billionaire businessman.

Rarely did my mother fuss over me anymore, nor did she use a tone of voice that demanded my attention.

Truth was, I could tell she was worried.

I forked a piece of the lasagna on my plate, and forced myself to chew and swallow it. I kept eating, and before I knew it, I'd cleaned the entire plate. Maybe I was hungry, but I hadn't really stopped to think about it.

I lifted my brow as I looked at her. She'd gotten both of us coffee, and had taken a seat across from me while I scarfed down a whole plate of Italian food. "Happy now?" I asked.

She shook her head. "No. You look like hell, Eli. But I'm glad you got some food in your belly."

I gave her a small, involuntary smile. My mother, Elizabeth Stone, was a force to be reckoned with in business. Although she'd slowed down after my father had passed away, doing more philanthropic work now, she'd worked side by side with my dad for decades. She was frighteningly intelligent and intuitive, plus she was well educated. My father had always seen her as one of his greatest assets, both in and out of business.

She'd definitely cut the umbilical cord a long time ago, but we were still close. With my dad gone now, Mom was all I had.

"It's not exactly been an easy couple of days, Mom."

"I expect it wasn't," she agreed. "I'm so sorry this happened, Eli. But I'm relieved that Jade is going to be okay."

My parent had listened to me talk about Jade, but I was grown, so I didn't talk much about my emotions with her anymore. "It was my fault," I confessed.

"It was an accident," she corrected.

"A fall that I caused," I rasped. "I saw her too close to the edge, and I yelled at her. I startled her, and she fell."

"You are *not* going to blame yourself for this," she insisted. "Accidents happen. You acted out of fear. And you had no intention of making her fall."

"It was stupid," I growled. "I don't act with my emotions. Ever."

I calculated almost everything, thought it through before I reacted. But Jade had turned my usually logical brain upside down.

"You're not a robot, son," she pointed out. "Somewhere along the way, you're going to have emotional reactions, no matter how much you try to avoid them."

"I don't want to feel this way," I said in a desperate voice.

"You care about her," she deduced. "I'm glad."

"I'm not. And I think I care too damn much."

My mom smiled. "Does she know that?"

"Hell, no."

"Maybe you should tell her."

"It wasn't part of the deal. And I've pretty much been a dick to her. She'd probably run the other direction if I told her I was having a change of heart about the *no commitment* thing."

"So you're going to do the running instead," she predicted. "Because she scares you."

I ran a frustrated hand through my hair. "Right now, I don't know what the fuck I'm doing, and I hate that."

My mom reached out and grabbed my hand. "Don't let the past mess up your future, Eli. It's been years. It's time to let it go. You should sell her the land."

"I can't," I croaked out. "You know I can't."

She shook her head. "I've watched you torture yourself for years. For entirely no reason. It has to stop."

It was a subject I absolutely *didn't* talk about, and today was no exception. "I want to focus on Jade right now," I told her.

"You're as stubborn as your father was," she lamented.

I crossed my arms. "Are you going to try to convince me that my orneriness only comes from him?"

"You think it comes from me?" she gasped, putting her hand to her chest with mock distress. "Not possible. I'm as sweet as a Georgia peach," she drawled, laying on her Southern accent.

I let out a reluctant grunt of laughter. My mother *could* be sweet, but she was by no means a Southern belle. She'd been out of the South for decades, and she'd learned to bite when necessary. Luckily, she had a kind heart.

"I'm sorry I'm being a jerk," I said, feeling bad because my mother had taken care of everything for me, and as always, she'd jumped into the fire with both feet.

I hadn't even noticed that she'd been trying to make things easier for all of Jade's family. Maybe it was because it was what my mom always did.

"It's just been a really tough few days," I added.

"You don't need to apologize. You're my son, Eli. I know you love me. But when you hurt, I hurt. All I ever want is to see you happy."

I saw the tears glistening in her eyes, and it jolted me into reality. "I know. Thanks for coming. But you need to go home and get some sleep. Is Jeff here to drive you home?"

She nodded.

"Good. Did *you* eat?"

"I did," she confirmed. "I had a lovely talk with Brooke while we were having dinner. If Jade is anything like her sister, she's a lovely girl. The Sinclairs are an amazing family. Their rags-to-riches story is pretty remarkable. But it hurts my heart to know how much they struggled. It must have been hard for Noah."

"I think it was difficult for all three of Jade's older brothers. But they're all pretty tough."

"You need a girl like her," my mother mused.

"Enough," I said gently. "Leave my love life to me."

She rose from the table. "If I left everything to you, I'd never live to see a grandchild," she said huffily.

"No guilt trips," I said. "You're not exactly elderly and on your deathbed."

My mother was still beautiful, and just as active as she'd always been. She could work circles around women who were decades younger.

I stood up, snagged her lightweight jacket, and held it out for her.

When she turned around, she gave me a worried look. "Please get some rest. I know you're not going to leave, but try to sleep."

I was my mother's son, and she knew it. When my father had been critically ill before he'd died, my mother had never left his side.

She continued, "I left you a bag of clothes in the closet." She pointed at the small wardrobe in the room. "There's a physician's shower around the corner. I'll be back tomorrow."

I nodded. Honestly, I was grateful for clean clothing. I was pretty sure I stank.

I hugged her tight for a moment and then watched her walk out the door.

I gathered up the clean clothes and went to find the shower.

My mother was right. I wasn't going anywhere. But for the sake of all Jade's family, I knew I needed to clean up.

I was back in her room ten minutes later, determined to camp out there until I was finally convinced that Jade was going to be okay.

CHAPTER 17

JADE

I woke up abruptly, panicked because I didn't know where I was or why I didn't recognize my surroundings.

"Where am I?" I called out in the dim light of what appeared to be a hospital room.

I gulped in deep breaths, trying to calm myself down, suddenly realizing that my whole body hurt.

"You're okay," Eli's steady voice said as he came to the side of the bed. "You had an accident, sweetheart."

Just his presence made my heart rate return to normal, and my fear dissolved when he reached out and grabbed my hand.

I remember. I was awake a few times. After I answered some questions for the nurse, I went right back to sleep.

Images of my fall from the rappel cliff flashed through my mind, followed by memories of excruciating pain. And then there was nothing. "I fell. All I remember is the pain," I told him softly. My throat and my mouth were dry. "Can I have some water?"

"You can have any damn thing you want now that you're talking to me," he said in a low, raspy voice.

He held the water glass, and I drank my fill from the straw before I asked, "Are we in Montana?"

"No. We're back in San Diego. You were flown to Billings first, and once you were stabilized, you were cleared to fly back here. You've been here for two days now. It's been almost five days since the accident. They're slowly cutting down your pain medication, so you'll probably be more awake now."

His face was close to mine after he sat down, and I squinted to see him. "You look awful," I said.

Eli's eyes were red, and his face looked ravaged with exhaustion.

He grinned at me. "You haven't seen yourself. I think you look a hell of a lot more beat up than I do."

"What did I injure?"

My whole body hurt, so I couldn't really pin down my real injuries.

"You bruised just about everything," he said grimly. "But the major stuff is a dislocated shoulder and you fractured your skull."

"And I thought that rappel was pretty tame," I muttered.

"It should have been. I'm so fucking sorry, Jade. I made you fall because I yelled at you. You would have been fine if I hadn't startled you."

A flash of memory revealed the moment when Eli had called out so loud that I'd faltered. "It wasn't your fault," I denied. "I was way too close to the edge. I saw a bald eagle, and I wanted a picture. I was already in an awkward position because I was trying to get my camera out. Being that unstable on the edge of a steep drop was my stupidity."

"That's why I yelled up to you. It was instinct. A bad one. You would have been okay if I hadn't made you completely lose your balance," he said stiffly.

I could hear the remorse in his voice, and I hated it. I reached out my hand to stroke his tight, whiskered jaw. "Don't blame yourself because I was dumb. It was an accident. I assume I'm going to live?"

He nodded. "It's going to take a couple of months for you to recover, but thank fuck you didn't do any lasting damage. But you're going to hurt."

"It's tolerable," I told him. Now that I was over the initial shock of waking up in pain, it didn't seem quite so bad anymore.

"Your head will heal. It was an uncomplicated linear fracture, so it will just take time. We were lucky."

I sighed and leaned back against the pillows. Honestly, I knew I'd gotten a break. An uncontrolled fall from that height could have done a lot more damage if I'd fallen on my head. "I'll live," I joked. "It's not the first time I've banged myself up."

"It's going to be the last," he grumbled.

"I'm sorry you were worried," I said. "Have you slept at all?"

"Yeah. Some. I had to fight your brothers and sister to sleep in the other bed, but I did sleep until you woke up."

"My family was here?"

"Did you really doubt it?" he teased. "The whole damn clan has been here, including your sister, Brooke."

"Brooke's here?" I asked excitedly.

"I doubt there was much that would keep her away when she heard you'd gotten hurt. She and Liam have been here since you got to San Diego. They only go home to sleep. I think your half-siblings and cousins would be here, too, but Noah talked them out of coming since you were stable. He said the room was full enough already."

I smiled. "That sounds like him," I acknowledged. "I feel bad that they've had to stop their lives to be here with me."

"Are you kidding? You know you would have done the same."

Eli was right. If any of my siblings were in the hospital, I would have camped out with them. "I guess I would."

"Honestly, I'm not sure we can get them to leave. My mom has been feeding them every single day. I have no idea what's on the menu for tomorrow, but I guarantee your brothers will be there when it gets here."

"Your mom was here?" I said, feeling slightly embarrassed that even Eli's mother had been hanging out in the hospital. "She probably hates me for making you so sleep deprived. You really don't look good."

"I feel a lot better now," he said huskily. "You scared the shit out of me, Butterfly."

If our positions were reversed, I knew I would have been terrified, too. "I'm sorry. I missed my last day in Montana. And I've pretty much spaced most of the last several days. All I can remember are images."

"You're probably better off that way," he said in a pained voice. "I'd *like* to forget. And Montana will still be there when you're feeling better. Although I'd much prefer you avoid it. You had way too many bad things happen there."

My heart ached as I saw the strain on his face and heard it in his voice. Eli looked like he'd been dragged through hell and back.

"How long do I have to stay in the hospital?" I asked.

"Until the doctor discharges you," he said firmly. "You'll probably be transferred to a regular room tomorrow. But your gorgeous ass is staying put in the hospital until you're ready to go home."

I knew I was going to have to be able to take care of myself. I refused to have my brothers babysit me. They'd eventually drive me crazy. "How long will I be in a sling?"

"At least a few weeks. And you won't have full use of that arm until the immobilizer is gone. Maybe longer. But it doesn't matter. You'll be staying with me."

"In San Diego?" I asked.

"Yes. And don't argue. You're going to need rechecks, and possibly physical therapy. It would be better if you're here."

My head was still fuzzy, and I wasn't sure whether I should disagree with him or not. I wanted to be with him, but I wasn't entirely sure that it was a good idea. "Our ten days are over."

"We're extending," he said roughly. "And I postponed the fund-raiser for your charity, but I didn't cancel it. It can wait until you're better."

I smiled at him. Well, as much as I was able to curve my lips. I was pretty sure I'd split my lip and it had been sutured.

Honestly, Eli's offer was so . . . unexpected. I wasn't sure what to say. True, he'd started out trying to get me into bed, but I'd never imagined that he'd turn out to be such a good man all the way around.

I knew he wasn't thinking about sex, considering the way I had to look at the moment.

"Thank you," I murmured.

"You can thank me when you're recovered," he grumbled.

"I think you should get some sleep," I said, worried about the lines of stress on his face.

He might be as gorgeous as ever, and he rocked the scruffy look with the stubble on his jaw, but I was pretty sure it wasn't intentional.

However, I hated the tormented look in his eyes, and the dead-tired lines that were scattered all over his face.

"I'll wait until you fall asleep," he rumbled.

"Stubborn," I said.

He smirked. "Been accused of that before."

"Will you really sleep after I do?" I asked skeptically.

"I promise."

"I'm glad you're here, Eli," I said as I closed my heavy eyelids.

"I'll *always* be here, Butterfly," he vowed.

I knew we were in extenuating circumstances, and people some-times made promises they didn't mean, but I sleepily hoped he was right.

CHAPTER 18

JADE

I was out of the hospital in two days, but it took two weeks for me to be free of the sling on my arm.

I'd gotten it off earlier in the morning, just in time for the gala that Eli's mom had rescheduled for my charity, SWCF.

I'd been staying at Eli's waterfront home in San Diego, a sleek, contemporary house with a ton of bedrooms and bathrooms. But what the house lacked in character was made up for by the stunning walls of windows and the water views.

I might hate the traffic and the city, but Eli had an amazing home.

"What in the hell are you doing?" Eli bellowed from the open door of the sitting room that was attached to the bedroom he'd put me in.

I was sitting in an awkward position on one of the small chairs, one leg bent up, and my foot on the edge of the seat. "Painting my toenails," I informed him without looking up.

We were due to attend the gala tonight, and I was making a special effort to look good. I'd spent most of the day with Skye. She'd come to San Diego for the day, and we went to have lunch, and then went shopping. She'd helped me pick out a new outfit since I had nothing appropriate for a party with a ton of rich people.

"You're supposed to be watching that shoulder. You're bending too much," he said in an annoyed tone.

As usual, Charlie was at Eli's heels, but he plopped down in the corner and proceeded to close his eyes to get a nap.

Honestly, I was getting used to Eli disapproving of every single physical thing I was doing. "I was cleared to resume normal activities," I reminded him.

He moved into the room and grabbed an ottoman, plopping it down right in front of me before he sat down. "Give me that," he ordered as he reached for the polish in my hand.

"Seriously?" I asked, putting the brush back in the bottle. I'd never had a guy offer to polish my toenails.

"Give it," he said as he pulled the bottle of Blackberry Red polish from my hand.

I watched as he wrapped his big hands around my foot and pulled it onto his lap.

"Oh, my God," I said with amazement. "You're really going to do it."

He shot me a warning look before he went to work polishing my toenails. "I've always thought it was kind of an awkward thing for women to do themselves anyway," he grumbled.

I leaned back in the chair. "It is. I hate it. But I'm wearing sandals, so I really have to paint my toenails."

There was no way I was going to put up a fight. It was kind of nice to watch Eli with his head bent, his attention focused on getting the polish on straight.

Really, it was one of the sweetest things anybody had ever done for me.

Not that Eli hadn't been an incredible caretaker during the last two weeks. He'd babied the crap out of me way too much.

I'd been uncomfortable at first when his mom had come over during the day when Eli was in the office. It was awkward in the beginning, and I told both of them over and over that I could take care of myself, but neither one of them was having it.

Over the course of the last two weeks, Elizabeth Stone and I had become friends. She was a woman of incredible business acumen, but she also had a heart of gold. Liz had taken over teaching me everything I needed to know about the business world during the day, so I was learning my way pretty fast. Obviously, it would take years for me to have the same understanding that she did, but I was starting to feel more comfortable with managing stuff myself.

"Shit!" Eli cursed as he got a tiny smear of polish on my skin.

I quietly handed him the nail-polish-remover towelettes. "It happens all the time."

He put his head back down and wiped the color off my skin, and then resumed what he'd been doing. I had to be honest, from what I could tell, he was doing a better job than I would have. When it came to nails, I got impatient and just slapped the color on without much regard to whether or not I had covered every single tiny portion of the nail.

But not Eli.

He was laser-focused on doing a good job. Maybe that was why he was so successful. He pretty much threw himself into doing everything well.

One thing I'd noticed about him in the last weeks was how he was in the moment, giving something his all, even if it was only a normal task.

The intense fixation that had once made me uncomfortable now fascinated me. The man could multitask, but he never lost sight of his original mission.

"I know you gave me a guest list, but what is the atmosphere going to be like? What do celebrities and billionaires talk about when they're out for the evening?"

I knew I was going to feel a little intimidated, but I wanted to be prepared.

The event was being held at some swanky country club, and a concert by some of the biggest names in music was going to follow the gala and dinner. I had no idea how Eli had talked those in-demand musicians into donating their time, but he said they had all refused payment.

Eli had convinced every one of them that it was a cause worth supporting.

He finally raised his head and put my painted foot carefully on the floor and lifted the other one. "What does anybody talk about? Their kids, vacations, hobbies, occasionally investments. Whatever comes to mind."

"I'm a little nervous," I confessed.

"Don't be," he answered. "They're there to help you."

"Don't think I don't appreciate that," I said hurriedly, not wanting him to think I wasn't grateful. "It's just a little daunting to attend a party that I never would have been invited to when I was poor."

"I would have invited you," he countered.

"If I hadn't come into money, we never would have met," I said thoughtfully. "We didn't exactly hang out in the same circles."

"Maybe," he confirmed. "But I think you'll find out that not everyone there is filthy rich. And many of them weren't born rich. Some are entrepreneurs who busted their asses to become successful, but they aren't billionaires."

"It's amazing that all of those people are supporting my charity. It's pretty humbling."

"Your report helped," he told me. "You have a talent for writing up the facts but making them personal."

I'd worked hard on getting information together for possible supporters. "Maybe because it's my passion."

"It shows," he said in a serious tone.

"The donations will help SWCF buy out some important corridors. Thank you."

"Don't thank me," he requested. "Now that I've seen all the information, I get why preserving those pieces of land and keeping them undeveloped is critical to wildlife. In some cases, you can already see some species being completely surrounded. I'm not sure why it was never thought about before development."

"It was, actually. But more often than not, big business wins out and the animals lose."

He lifted his head and looked at me with a grin. "Not anymore. The more backing you get, the more weight you can throw around."

Eli gently put my foot on the floor, capped the polish, and handed it back to me. "All done."

"You're an angel," I said with a sigh. "Thanks. Not that you needed to do it, but they look so much better than what I would have done."

I gently flexed my feet and wiggled my toes. Eli had done an expert job.

"I'm definitely *not* an angel," he argued. "And how do you know that I didn't do it just so that I could touch you?"

My heart tripped. Eli hadn't so much as made *any* personal comments in the last two weeks. He'd been way too concerned about making sure I did everything the doctor ordered.

But I was cleared now. I had some simple exercises I could do for the next several weeks to build my shoulder back up slowly, but I didn't even need to go to physical therapy.

"You can touch me now," I informed him in a tremulous voice. "I'm recovered."

The sexual tension between me and Eli was always there, always present. As I started to feel better, the intensity had ramped right back up to where it used to be, maybe even more urgent.

Being close to him now without any physical contact was absolutely agonizing.

"I'm not compromising your recovery just to get laid," he said roughly. "If you get too much activity too soon, it will put you back to where you were two weeks ago."

I could still see the desire in Eli's beautiful, stormy eyes, so I knew he was feeling the unbearable chemical attraction, too. "Then just kiss me," I said, frustrated.

Eli put both of his hands on the chair, pinning me in as he leaned down close. "I think we both know where that would lead," he said hoarsely. "I can't touch you without wanting to fuck you until neither one of us can move."

God, I wanted that, too. So badly that my body physically ached for him. "One kiss," I requested.

His eyes turned a deeper gray, and they were smoldering with fire. "You know damn well I can't say no."

I probably did know it, but if Eli didn't touch me in some way, I was going to go crazy.

He put his fingers under my chin, tilted my head up, and his mouth captured mine in less than a heartbeat.

The delicious heat and power of his embrace made me sigh against his lips.

I savored the intimacy as he thoroughly explored my mouth, the kiss so blazing hot that I felt like I was going to incinerate.

I desperately wanted to wrap my arms around his neck and grasp his coarse hair, keeping him close to me. But I was afraid it would cut short the closeness between us, and I wanted to relish every stroke of his tongue.

Eli didn't just kiss; he claimed. His alpha-male tendencies didn't make me uncomfortable anymore. In fact, sometimes I craved them because I wanted him with the same fierceness, and I got as locked up into the craziness of our desire as he did.

When he finally lifted his head, I bit back a protest. I didn't want him to move away.

But he did.

Eli straightened and strode to the door.

"Get ready, Jade," he said in a hoarse voice. "We have to leave in an hour."

"I know," I answered, still trying to catch my breath.

He snapped his fingers for Charlie to follow him. "Let's go, buddy," he said to the canine. "If I can't see her naked, you're not going to either."

I laughed because I knew he was teasing in a moment filled with deprivation.

"I never said you couldn't watch," I said playfully.

His back was to me as he answered, "If I did, we'd never get to the fund-raiser."

Man and dog both exited the room without another sound.

CHAPTER 19

ELI

I have to get some fucking control!

I slumped against the shower tile, the powerful jets from the shower pounding against my back. The proof that I'd just jacked off again and found release was circling the drain, and then disappearing like my orgasm had never happened.

And for the most part, it didn't matter, because my dick didn't feel better. I didn't feel any damn better.

Getting myself off wasn't helping anymore.

I wanted one thing, and one thing only.

Jade.

Goddammit!

My dick wasn't settling for easy imitations anymore.

I grabbed a bottle of shampoo and roughly worked at soaping up my hair, irritated that I didn't have enough discipline to keep my hands off her.

She was just cleared to go back to regular activity.

But that didn't mean she could put a ton of stress on her shoulder. She was very limited as far as how much stress and how much weight she could handle. And it wasn't much.

During her recovery, my lunatic desire had taken a break. I'd been too damn worried about making sure that she didn't having any lasting effects from her fall.

The bruises, scrapes, and lacerations on her face were pretty much healed, but the accident itself was the subject of almost every one of my nightmares.

This shit has to stop!

I'd caused her fall because of my fear that something was going to happen to her, and I was no damn good for Jade. I'd caused her too much pain already, and I wasn't willing to risk having it happen again because I couldn't control my instincts when I was around her.

I was fucked up, and I knew it. And for reasons that had nothing to do with her.

I fucking hurt her! I could have killed her because of my insane desire to protect her.

I'd been convincing myself for two weeks that she was better off without me, and I was almost persuaded that I was right.

Kissing her had been a compulsion I hadn't been able to resist.

But I was absolutely *not* doing it again.

My guilt over her fall had nearly killed me, and I honestly wasn't certain that I could go through that again.

The pain.

The terror.

The paralyzing remorse.

Every emotion had eaten me alive while she'd been recovering.

My nightmares had been real, and I never slept after I'd had one. I was too damn agitated to go back to sleep.

I rinsed myself, slammed the shower off, and got out to dry myself.

I cared too damn much, and I was no longer willing to deny it. And that made Jade a danger to my sanity.

If I fuck her, I'm done.

As hard as it was going to be, I *had* to cut her out of my life.

I'd get over *it*.

I'd get over *her*.

And she'd be safe because I wouldn't be there to screw up her life.

If she was no longer around, she'd fade away and eventually just be a distant memory.

My chest ached, and I felt empty. In a matter of weeks, Jade Sinclair had turned my whole world upside down.

I needed it upright again.

I had to sleep. I had to eat. I had to not have a damn erection every single moment I spent with her.

My life was all about order and balance. I had too much responsibility not to maintain a cool head.

I tossed the used towel into the hamper and walked into my bedroom buck naked, knowing I didn't have long to get ready for the gala.

My tux had already been hung on the door of the closet, so I reached inside a drawer to get a pair of boxer briefs.

As I pulled out the underwear, my eyes landed on a little red box that I'd put there soon after I'd brought Jade home from the hospital.

I wanted to just slam the drawer closed, but I couldn't. So I picked up the box, and as I opened the lid, I felt my chest squeeze inside my sternum.

After the accident, I'd had a moment of temporary insanity and I'd bought the ring.

I'd thought I was ready to make a commitment because I hadn't been able to imagine a life without her anymore.

The large diamond in a platinum setting was bright and fiery. It had reminded me of her.

I can't do it. I can't.

Nothing I felt about Jade was the slightest bit rational. I'd do something stupid again, and I'd hurt her. Yeah. Maybe I wouldn't mean to, but there's no coming back from death.

God knew that nobody understood that better than I did.

I wasn't thinking about all the ramifications of a relationship when I bought this ring.

I slammed the lid closed.

"What in the hell was I thinking?" I muttered in a graveled voice.

I stuffed the box into the back of the drawer.

Not. Happening.

I was not going to marry her, and I sure as hell wasn't going to stay around to make her life miserable.

I slammed the drawer closed.

Jade didn't need a ring.

She needed a man who was always going to be there, somebody who wasn't going to go bat-shit crazy if she so much as tore a fingernail.

That kind of behavior wasn't normal.

It wasn't healthy.

And it sure as hell wasn't rational.

I need to get my control back.

I was also going to need some distance. It was the only thing that was going to help.

Jade wasn't the type of woman any guy could walk away from easily.

She's going back home tomorrow.

And damned if just the thought of not having her in my life all the time brought up an answering protest that I felt deep in my gut. In fact, it fucking hurt so bad I could barely breathe.

"Shit!" I rasped. "I'm so fucked."

I walked into the bathroom to shave, trying desperately not to think about what was going to happen.

Because honestly, I had no idea how I was ever going to walk away from Jade.

CHAPTER 20

Jade

"A little more at the corner of your eye," Brooke instructed me as she watched me apply my makeup in the mirror via an Internet video chat.

It had taken some doing, but I'd managed to get my laptop set at an angle where she could help me figure out all this makeup stuff.

I flicked the brush lightly in the corner of my eye. "When did makeup become a damn science?" I asked her.

We'd gone through a painstaking process of doing an evening makeup job, and I wasn't sure I liked it.

Sure, I occasionally put on a little lipstick, and maybe some mascara, but for the most part, I wore nothing because I was outside in the middle of nowhere in all different kinds of weather. Generally, none of the stuff I was piling on my face worked in my usual environments.

Brooke laughed. "Honestly, I don't usually fuss with that much makeup, either. But one of the local ladies had a class at the rec center, and I learned a lot. I'm trying to share my knowledge with you. You said you wanted to look good."

I sighed. "I do."

Brooke talked me through the rest of the process, and when I finally stepped back, I was reasonably satisfied. "I guess this is as good as it gets," I told my twin.

"Turn," she requested.

I turned around and took off the towel I was wearing like a bib to keep any stray makeup off my dress, and then stepped back so she could see me.

"Perfect," she said. "You look beautiful, Jade."

I moved to the desk, put the computer down, and sat in front of the screen. "Are you sure? Don't you think it's a little over the top?"

Brooke made a face. "Absolutely not," she argued. "Not everybody can rock that dress the way you do, and it's a dinner and cocktail party full of rich people who are going to dress up. You look amazing."

Skye had talked me into the black cocktail dress. She said it was sexy without being slutty. It was fitted, so it clung pretty tight to my body, but with the round neck and the cowl that hung down low in the back, it was also elegant. I loved the black lacy sleeves that were snug on my arms, but not too tight. The hem hit right above the knee.

"I'm not used to wearing a dress," I told Brooke.

"You wore one at my wedding," she reminded me.

"I did that for you," I mumbled.

"Then wear this one for yourself," she insisted. "Or are you doing it for Eli?"

"Maybe a little of both," I conceded. "He pulled all this together for me. I want to look nice."

"Sister, you look better than nice," Brooke answered. "He'll be drooling all night."

Did I want Eli to drool? Yeah, it was quite possible that I did.

"He's barely touched me since the accident," I admitted. "I guess maybe I want to get his attention, too."

"Oh, Jade. You already have it," she assured me. "If you could have seen how upset he was when you were hurt, you'd know that. The guy hardly ate or slept."

"I know. I could see that after my drugs wore off. But he's been different, Brooke. I don't know how to explain it, but he's . . . distant."

"You were recovering from some major trauma," she pointed out.

I couldn't exactly put a finger on the difference, but it worried me. "I hope you're right."

"Do you love him?" she asked in a rush. "No, wait. I'm your twin. I know you do."

I nodded slowly. "I do. I'm not sure when it happened, but it scares the hell out of me."

"I know he feels the same way, so I'm not worried. The fear goes away, Jade," she said softly. "I promise."

"He made it clear that he wanted me in his bed, Brooke. But emotions weren't part of the deal. He's not the type of guy who wants any commitments. He already told me that."

"He's full of shit," Brooke answered. "Eli Stone is so in love with you that he can't think straight. Maybe this all started as a game or a fling, but somewhere along the way, everything changed."

"For me it definitely did," I confessed.

"For him, too," she insisted. "Things don't always work out the way you plan them, but that's the best part of life. The surprises."

"Like Liam?" I asked with a smile. I adored my twin's husband, but I couldn't help but wish that he had lived in California.

Brooke's face softened, and her eyes danced just from hearing his name. "Liam and I shouldn't have worked out at all. But somehow I think I always knew that he was the only guy I was ever going to love. It starts as lust, and then . . . bam! I couldn't live without him anymore."

"He makes you happy," I said.

"Very," she confirmed.

"I really want to hate him because he took you across the country from me, but I can't," I told her.

"It doesn't matter," she said. "We'll always be there for each other. When you got hurt, Liam was the one who packed the bags while I freaked out. But there was no question as to whether or not I was going. He gets that, and he wanted to be there, too. Liam is special that way. When I need him, he's just there without question."

"At least getting to see each other isn't an issue when we have access to private jets," I joked.

"Exactly," she said. "And now that I'm back from traveling, we'll talk to each other all the time. I miss all of you."

"We miss you, too," I said tearfully.

"Don't start crying," she warned. "All that makeup will run."

I blinked furiously to keep from leaking any tears from my eyes. "I've got it under control."

"Have fun, Jade. And enjoy your night with a really hot guy. You'll be the envy of most single women around the world."

I groaned. "Oh, God. I never even thought about that."

To me, he was just Eli. To everybody else, he was the most eligible bachelor in the world.

She laughed. "Don't think about it, then."

We kept things light before we finally said good-bye.

And for the first time, I ended my conversation with my twin without being really sad.

Yeah, sometimes I felt Brooke's absence, but I knew that no matter how many miles separated us, we'd always have that twin bond that could never be broken.

And we could breach that distance any time we needed to see each other or spend time together.

Our inheritance had made flying across the country pretty easy.

"Hey, you ready?" I heard Eli's baritone ask as he came through the sitting room.

I stood, feeling nervous as hell in a skin I wasn't quite used to.

"Oh, my God," I said breathlessly as he appeared in the small powder room.

I'd been so busy being self-conscious that I hadn't even thought about the fact that Eli would be nicely dressed, too.

I already knew he was breathtaking in a suit.

But I wasn't prepared to see him in a tuxedo.

"You look . . . perfect," I murmured.

Eli reminded me of a certain sweet that a person craves. You know it isn't exactly good for you, but you want it just the same. He was pure temptation, and I knew I wasn't going to be able to not take more than just one bite.

He wore a tuxedo just like he wore a custom suit. He looked comfortable in formal wear, and he wore it with an elegance and sophistication that most guys could never quite pull off.

"Jesus, Jade," he said in a raspy, low voice when he came to a stop in front of me. "Are you trying to kill me?"

"No," I answered honestly. "I was trying to make sure I looked good on the arm of the hottest man at the party."

"You look beautiful," he said, his tone not completely happy. "What did you do to your hair?"

I turned, showing him the upswept style that Skye had taught me to do. "Cocktail-party hair."

It was a fairly easy pattern that was held in place by a giant silver clip, and left some tendrils curling along the side of my face.

"It makes me want to pull it out so I can feel it," he said hoarsely.

I turned back to him. "I think that's the idea," I responded lightly.

"And that dress is going to fuck with my mind all damn night."

"I'm covered," I said, secretly adoring the look of lust in his gorgeous, stormy eyes as they moved covetously down my body before they traveled up again to my face.

"Let's go," he rumbled as he took my hand.

His statement was abrupt, but I didn't take offense as I grabbed my little black bag. I smiled as I followed him as fast as my stiletto heels would allow me to move, knowing my objective of looking good on his arm had been achieved.

CHAPTER 21

JADE

We'd been at the party for over an hour, and everyone was still staring in our direction. Eli hadn't left my side, and we'd attacked the buffet full of food together.

I'd had more than one drink to try to relax. But it hadn't helped all that much.

"I feel like I'm in a fishbowl," I said to Eli as we mingled. "Everyone is watching you."

Just like he'd promised, he'd introduced me to so many people that I'd already forgotten most of their names.

He leaned in closer. "They aren't looking at *me*," he answered. "They're all looking at *you*."

"Thanks," I answered. "That makes me feel so much better."

"You'll get used to it. The interest in a new billionaire among their ranks wears off, and they move on to the next unfamiliar person who shows up. It hasn't been all that bad, right?"

Had it been all that bad? I guess it hadn't been as big of a nightmare as I'd assumed. "Not bad," I agreed. "So many of these people have the same concerns as everyone else I know. And I'm amazed at how many of them already donate to conservation causes."

He grinned. "I won't say that I told you so."

"But you want to," I said with an answering smile. "And I have no problem telling you that you were right."

Curious stares aside, the majority of the people I'd met talked about their spouses, their kids, and their causes first. It wasn't that they weren't discussing billion-dollar deals, but it was all part of the general conversation, just like any person would discuss their jobs. It just so happened that these folks dealt in much bigger dollars than most when it came to their businesses.

"If I steered you away from somebody, it was for a good reason. Just like any other group of people, not everybody is nice," he warned.

"That's true at almost any get-together," I observed.

He nodded. "But there's definitely more than a few guests here tonight that have pretty sharp claws."

"If you're trying to warn me about your previous girlfriends, I've already seen them," I said with a frown.

There were megarich businessmen everywhere, but I'd recognized some faces of celebrities as we'd worked our way around the large venue. Of course, I couldn't help but notice that more than a few of the gorgeous women here had once been on Eli's arm—in just the same position I was at the moment.

"None of them were girlfriends," he denied.

"Then what were they?"

"Arrangements," he answered in a clipped voice. "They wanted the same thing I did."

I shook my head slowly. "I don't think they did. Most of them are among the people staring. And those women are looking at both of us. Did you break it off when you got bored?"

For so many reasons, I wasn't sure I wanted to hear his response.

"Yes."

That one simple word made my heart stutter. Maybe Eli and I had become friends of a sort, but I wasn't any safer than any of the other women he'd gotten bored with in the past.

This was never meant to be long term. I accepted that. So I'm going to have to play by the rules.

I was silent for a moment as I stared out into the crowd.

Finally, I leaned into him so my mouth was close to his ear. "Promise me that you'll tell me when this is over," I requested softly. "I'd rather we stay friends."

I didn't want to be the woman he'd once dumped if we met up somewhere after our time together was over. I didn't want there to be a time when we couldn't meet up with no regrets on either side.

He leaned closer. "I can't be your friend, Jade. I can *never* be your friend."

My heart sank. The conviction in his voice was real. Nothing was ever going to come of this dysfunctional relationship I had with Eli. Like he intended, it was going to be a mutually pleasurable arrangement until one or both of us decided we didn't want it anymore.

"Okay," I said in a quiet voice as I glanced up at him.

Maybe I was imagining things, but I swore I saw a brief expression of vulnerable indecision in his eyes before it promptly disappeared. "Jade, I—"

"Don't," I interrupted him. "We both knew what we were getting into from the beginning. You made yourself perfectly clear. No commitments. And I was the one who decided to accept it."

I didn't want his sympathy because I'd gone and fallen for him just like the other women in the room who were gawking at him with longing expressions.

I didn't want to join that club.

I'd deal with my disappointment alone.

I *had* known the deal when I'd signed up for intimacy with Eli. But maybe in my heart I had hoped that it would change.

"Hey, Eli," a male voice called out.

I looked to see who was trying to get Eli's attention, and saw a guy around Eli's age approaching us.

The blond man didn't look nearly as elegant and aloof as Eli. In fact, he kind of reminded me of a carefree beach bum who just happened upon the party and dropped in for a drink.

My eyes went from the male who had just stopped in front of us, to the grim expression on Eli's face. It was obvious to me that Eli wasn't happy to see this particular guest.

"Joel," Eli acknowledged curtly.

I could feel the tension between the two males facing each other, but I couldn't figure out the cause.

"I just stopped by to give these to you," Joel told Eli as he held out a large manila envelope.

I waited for several heartbeats, stressful moments that kept ticking like a clock.

Eli made no move to accept the man's offering.

But the giver of the envelope also didn't seem like he was going to slink away.

Without thinking, I reached out and snatched the package from Joel's hand because I could see the tortured expression on Eli's face, and I couldn't take it anymore.

"Thanks," I said abruptly, willing to do almost anything to vanquish the tormented look in Eli's eyes.

Joel turned, smiled sadly at me, and then quickly retreated into the crowd.

"What's in this?" I asked Eli. "What's wrong?"

"I don't really know what it is, and I don't care," Eli said in an agitated tone. "Leave it. Throw it away. I don't give a fuck."

I fingered the envelope, and I couldn't help but notice that it was lightweight, but the contents felt like very substantial cardboard or a similar material. "Can I open it?"

I sensed that it wouldn't be wise to just trash the contents.

I took the complete silence from Eli as permission, and I slowly opened the envelope.

Surprised, I glanced at the photos that appeared to be of Eli.

Eli mountain climbing.

Eli fishing.

Eli skydiving.

By the time I flipped to the last picture, I was wondering why I never saw him smile the way he was doing in all of the photos.

I frowned as I viewed the last one.

Two men were standing side by side, and they were mirror images of each other.

One was Eli without his tribal tattoo.

And the other was Eli with the markings he had now.

"I don't understand," I said to myself as I traced the marks with my finger. "Are these both you?"

I recognized Eli's grin, but it wasn't on the face of the man with the tat.

Was the image some kind of double-image photography?

"Are they both you?" I mumbled again.

My escort finally broke his silence as he turned his hardened expression to the photo I was holding.

"No, they aren't both me," he said harshly. "This is me." He tapped the picture of the man without the tats.

"Then who is this?" I asked as I pointed to the other guy.

I was seriously confused. The two guys were identical, but I'd been able to recognize Eli's smile.

"The other man is my brother, Austin," he said in a low, dangerous tone. "He was my identical twin."

"Where is he now?" I asked in a tremulous voice.

"Dead. He died almost four years ago," Eli said in a raspy voice.

I nearly dropped the envelope as I hurriedly returned the pictures to the envelope, my heart squeezing like it was in a vise as I took Eli's hand and led him toward the exit.

CHAPTER 22

JADE

My heart was still racing even after Eli had silently driven us back to his place.

I couldn't seem to catch my breath as we walked inside his modern beach house. "Tell me what happened, Eli. Please."

Maybe most of the people at the cocktail party hadn't seen or felt the pain I could sense coming from Eli. I hurt because I knew that he hurt. I wasn't sure why it was happening, but I could experience his emotional pain, and feel it like it was my own.

Maybe it was because I knew what it was like to be bonded to a twin, and I couldn't even imagine living through the death of my sister.

I followed Eli as he shrugged out of his black tuxedo jacket, dropped it on the dining-room chair as he passed through, and proceeded to the living room to fix himself a drink.

He didn't bother to even take ice from the bar. He just turned up a tumbler and poured a significant amount of Scotch into the glass.

I reached around him and got into the fridge to pour myself a glass of wine, then sat on the couch.

"I don't talk about Austin," he said with a growl. "Never."

I breathed out a sigh of relief as he sat across from me in a chair. I kicked off the heels I was wearing and drew my legs up in front of me. "How can you not talk about it?" I asked, desperately hoping he'd tell me what happened.

It was pretty plain to me that Eli *was* haunted. I could see the lost look in his eyes even now.

He gulped down half of the glass of fine whisky before he answered roughly, "It happened four years ago. Joel was Austin's best friend. He was a photographer, so he apparently thought I'd want the pictures. End of story."

I could hear the warning in his voice, but I wasn't going to stop pushing. I knew in my heart that he needed to talk about his twin. Everything made sense to me now. He still needed to accept his brother's death, no matter how painful it might be to get there. "How did he die? He must have been young."

"Young and stupid," he replied sharply.

Eli looked up at me and continued, "Austin and I were close, just as tight as you and Brooke are now. But shit happened after we went away to different colleges."

He gulped down the rest of his drink and went to get another. I took a sip of my wine and waited. I'd sit on the couch the whole night if that's how long it took Eli to tell me everything.

He sat back down, his glass filled almost to the rim this time. "If you want the whole damn story, I'll tell it," he said huskily. "And then I never want to talk about it again."

I nodded, but didn't say a word.

"Austin was sixteen minutes older than I was, and he was the heir apparent to my father's businesses and fortune. Not that I wouldn't get my share, but it was always assumed he'd be living this life, not me. And I didn't give a damn. I never wanted this. I never wanted the attention. My dream as a kid had always been space technology, and I happily went away to Caltech to get my PhD. I didn't really want to run the family business, so I was glad that Austin was prepared to go off to Harvard and get his business degree."

"Did you get your degree?" I asked breathlessly, stunned by the fact that Eli had wanted to be a real rocket scientist. And maybe I was a bit in awe since Caltech was so damn hard to get into.

He nodded right before he took another gulp of his drink and kept talking. "I'd just finished my PhD when Austin died."

"I'm so sorry," I answered in a rush. "What happened?"

"Austin and I were always different. He was always in the limelight because he was a lot more social than I was. There wasn't anything Austin wouldn't do to get attention. And I idolized him because I was the shier kid. I was the quiet reader, and Austin was always the sports fanatic, an interest that my dad shared. So the two of them spent a lot of time together watching games and participating in different sports events."

"Did you feel left out?" I queried softly.

He shook his head. "No. My dad made sure we did other things together. I know that he loved me just as much as he loved Austin. But my brother was always the bright light, and I was pretty much the science geek."

Eli was like me.

It was pretty hard to imagine him being socially awkward, but it was possible that he'd grown into the role that he occupied today.

"You're not a geek anymore," I reassured him.

He shrugged. "Like I said, I didn't care. I was more than happy to sit back and let Austin be the outgoing brother. I was content with my own fate. In fact, it was what I desperately wanted."

"Were you close in college?" Obviously, they weren't together, but that didn't mean they didn't talk. And since money wasn't an issue, they could be together as much as they wanted when class was out.

"We were at first," he answered. "But after the first year or two, Austin got pretty wild. He started to fail out of his classes, and every time he called me, he was wasted. He ran with a crazy, rich crowd at Harvard. Drinking, women, drugs, and partying became his major, and no matter how many times I talked to him about it, nothing changed. My parents would send him to rehab, he'd go back to campus, and sooner or later, he'd fall off the wagon again. After five years on the East Coast, my dad just brought him back to California. I think he figured he could straighten him out if he was at home."

"But he didn't get better?" I asked.

"Sometimes he did," Eli said hoarsely. "Hell, there were times we thought he was going to straighten out. Maybe that was the hard part. We'd all start to feel optimistic, and then we'd get slammed over the head again when he disappeared. We knew he was on a binge. But he eventually came home again."

Until one day he didn't.

I already knew the story had an unhappy ending, but I waited to hear how his brother had died.

"I got to San Diego as much as I could," Eli explained. "But it wasn't enough. Near the end, Austin was doing some stupid shit. Almost like he had a death wish. It was never me who liked to go mountain climbing, to race cars, and to take up any extreme challenge that came my way. I had some hobbies, but after I'd worked that damn hard in college, I wanted to do something with my education."

"So those things were never your idea?"

No wonder the Eli I knew and the one who did all things crazy had never seemed to jibe.

"Not my thing," he admitted. "I guess I could always think of something better to do. My free time was at a premium. Not that Austin didn't ask, but I was usually busy with my studies. Now I guess I do them to keep his memory alive."

I let out a breath I hadn't even realized I'd been holding. "It isn't your fault, Eli," I said firmly.

When he'd said his visits home weren't enough, I knew he was blaming himself.

"I was his twin brother, for fuck's sake," he cursed, and then downed a little more of his drink. "I should have been there more, even if I had to do all his crazy shit along with him. It's fucked up that I only started seriously pursuing those things after he died."

Actually, it *wasn't* so crazy. Eli had been feeling the pain of being cut off from his twin, and he'd wanted to somehow find a way to keep Austin alive. He'd done that by twisting himself into his brother.

He nodded to the envelope in my hand as he explained, "That picture of the two of us at one of his auto races was the last time we were ever together. It was the summer after I'd finished my doctorate. He gave me hell all the time about being boring and not living my life. We'd started to spend more time together, and I was fucking determined to get his ass straightened out, even if I had to climb mountains and learn to hang glide."

I felt my eyes well up with tears. I tried to keep them in check. I knew it wasn't the end of the story. But it was killing me to think about Eli trying so hard to get close to his brother but being unable to save Austin.

I watched as Eli drained his glass and slammed it on the end table next to him. "My brother used to tell me to *keep the crazy going*. It was pretty much his motto in life. 'Keep the crazy going, bro.' It was the last thing he said to me the day before he died."

My heart sank. Eli had obviously taken his brother's words to heart, and he'd spun himself into a man he really wasn't to keep the memory of his brother alive.

The tattooed arm.

The crazy stunts.

The extreme challenges.

Taking over his father's company.

Everything Eli had done since he'd lost his identical twin revolved around making himself into two men. His brother, and himself.

In some ways, I got why he was doing it. Lord knew I would have done anything I could to deny the fact that I'd lost Brooke. But I couldn't really imagine it because I hadn't had to live through it like Eli had.

"You don't have to be Austin," I told him gently. "I think you can honor his memory without turning into a version of both of you."

Eli glared at me. "He asked for it. He wanted me to keep the crazy going."

If my sister had asked something specific of me, maybe I would have done the same thing. But I think it was time that Eli stopped trying to be anybody except himself.

The tears let loose, and I let them fall. My heart was aching, and it was the only way I could lessen the pain. "I don't think he meant it that way. How did he die?"

"Austin loved the property that you wanted to buy from me. It was a perfect party spot. Nobody around. No cops to bust him for illegal drugs. No problems with any excessive noise from his crazy party friends, like Joel and the rest of the gang from college. Joel and a few other guys were from California, so the party didn't end when my dad pulled Austin back home. Only the location had changed."

My heart was in my throat, but I forced two words from my mouth. "What happened?"

"Another party out on the family property. To this day, we aren't quite sure what happened. Joel and Austin's other buddies had passed out. They found him at the bottom of a cliff the next morning. Austin fell and broke his neck."

I stifled a sob by biting my lip.

Eli finally looked me directly in the eyes as he finished. "You want to know why I won't sell you that useless piece of land? Maybe because it's *not* useless to me. My brother died there, Jade. He spent his last moments teetering on a ledge, probably high and completely drunk, before he fell to his death. But I can't let go of the property, because my brother spent his last moments on Earth there. I hate the damn place, but I can't fucking let it go."

The reason why he'd freaked out when he saw me on the edge of the rappelling cliff made sense to me now. He *had* been terrified, and it was because he'd already lost somebody he cared about to a reckless fall. And just like he'd done with his brother, he blamed himself for my accident.

I gave up trying to pretend that my heart wasn't breaking for Eli. I stumbled to my feet, walked over to him, and dropped into his lap so I could wrap my arms around his shuddering body.

He lowered his head, and I put mine on top of his. I comforted the most ballsy man I knew while he wept.

CHAPTER 23

JADE

I had no idea whether Eli would have let himself be vulnerable if he hadn't downed a significant amount of whisky, but it really didn't matter.

Somehow, I knew he needed to grieve, and to sort out the jumble of emotions he'd held inside for too damn long.

My tears flowed, most of them being absorbed by Eli's white shirt, while I held on to him like my life depended on it.

I squeaked as he finally composed himself and rose with my body cradled in his arms. "What are you doing?" I asked in a surprised tone.

He lowered me to my feet slowly, and then proceeded to dry the tears that were still pouring down my cheeks. When he was done, he palmed the side of my face, stroking a thumb down my cheek as he said huskily, "I'm about to find out where the zipper of this dress is hidden."

My heart skittered as I saw his eyes turn smoky and dark. "I know where it is," I informed him in a breathless voice.

Deep inside, I probably knew that it wasn't a good idea to be physically intimate with Eli, but I'd waited so long for him that I wasn't going to say no.

With Eli, I was either all in or all out. There was no halfway with this man.

"Then I suggest you tell me where it is before I ruin this dress," he warned.

His large hands sank into my hair, causing the clip to fall out and my confined locks to tumble to my shoulders.

"Better," he said with satisfaction, just before his mouth came down hard on mine.

I was lost from the moment our lips touched.

I was done not giving Eli everything I had to give. I was in love with him, and as scary as those emotions might be, I wasn't going to run away.

I wanted him too damn much.

Yes, I'd probably eventually lose him, because that was our deal. But I was going to see exactly how it felt to be with somebody I loved.

My arms snaked around his neck, and my fingers found their way into the coarse strands of his hair.

I whimpered against his mouth, my body demanding so much more.

"Eli," I moaned as he released my lips.

I let my head fall back, savoring the feel of his hungry kiss on the sensitive skin of my neck.

Every sensible thought I had flew out of my brain as Eli permeated every cell in my body.

I had no control, nor did I want it. All I wanted was to let myself drown in Eli's hot, sensual touch.

He bit down gently on the skin of my neck, and then rolled his tongue over the sting. The erotic sensation sent me completely over the edge.

I tried to wedge my arms between us to get the shirt off his body. *I need to touch him. I have to touch him.*

My movements were so frantic that Eli stepped back and took off his shirt before dumping it onto the floor.

My mouth went dry. Eli Stone was probably the most perfectly built man on the planet, and for the moment, he was mine.

I moved forward and ran my hands down his muscular chest, my fingers nearly burning from the scorching heat of his silken skin. He was throwing off warmth like a furnace, and I was more than happy to let myself fall into that fire.

I raised my head to look at him. "You're perfect," I blurted out.

The intensity of his stare made my heart start to race. I could feel the same longing I was experiencing reflected back to me in his eyes.

His gaze locked with mine, he expertly found the hidden zipper of my dress and lowered it. I held my breath as he kept me pinned in place only with his gaze.

He tugged, and I helped him pull the dress down my body. His breath caught as the material cleared my bare breasts. I didn't stop. I just wiggled the material down my legs until I was standing in front of him in a pair of panties and my thigh-high stockings.

"Nice panties," he remarked huskily.

They were the black pair he'd given to me at the resort. "They were a gift," I answered in a shaky voice.

"Jesus, Jade. I want you so damn much that it almost hurts just to look at you."

Liquid heat rushed between my thighs, so I knew exactly what he meant. My core clenched, and my body was pleading with me to ease the ache.

I wrapped my arms around him. "Then let's make the pain stop," I suggested in a low, sensual tone. "Because I hurt, too."

"I never wanted to hurt you," he rasped.

"Then fuck me, Eli," I pleaded.

An animal-like sound came out of his mouth as he lowered his head to kiss me, and I savored his desire.

His embrace was ravenous, but he teased my lips with his teeth, and then devoured them again. He repeated the same actions over and over again, teasing until I wanted to scream at him to fuck me.

I rubbed my body shamelessly against his, reveling in the feel of his bare skin against my diamond-hard nipples.

"I need more, Eli," I whimpered when he'd finally lifted his head.

"You'll get more, Butterfly," he answered gruffly. "Probably more than you want. But I need to find condoms."

"I'm on birth control. Now," I insisted, reaching for his pants.

"Not yet," he commanded, grabbing my wrist to keep me from freeing his cock. "I want both of us to enjoy this, and I'm not going to last very long."

"I don't care," I told him defiantly.

"I care," he growled as he gripped my panties and yanked them off with one hard pull. "Jump up."

I quickly obeyed, hopping up enough to wrap my legs around his waist as my torn undies fell to the floor.

I shuddered as I tightened my legs around his waist and pressed my lower body forward until my sex met his hot skin. "Yes," I hissed, gyrating against his rock-hard body.

I sighed as I absorbed the feel of our bodies meeting skin-to-skin, and my pussy pressed up against the outline of his erect cock.

Eli's hands grasped my ass and pulled me even tighter against him, and then moved to the nearest wall to prop my back up.

"Dammit!" he cursed, his fist slamming against the wall over my head. "I have no control when it comes to you."

"You don't need it," I whispered in his ear. "You'll never need it with me."

My words must have sunk in, because I could feel Eli freeing himself, and I shivered in anticipation.

His impatience was evident when he sheathed himself inside me with one powerful lunge.

I panted and speared my hands into his hair. Eli was a big man, and the stretching sensation of having him buried to his balls inside me was slightly painful. But the satisfaction of being joined intimately with him was so much more earth-shattering than the twinge of pain.

"Yes. God, Eli, I've wanted this for so long," I confessed.

He grunted. "Probably not nearly as long as I have."

The pain faded away, and all that was left was the carnal pleasure of Eli squeezing my ass cheeks as he pulled out and plunged back into me again.

I held on to him, and he set a punishing rhythm, one that threatened to make me lose my mind.

He gripped my ass so hard I knew I'd probably have his finger marks on my butt cheeks, but his hold also helped me move to meet him on every stroke. My hips moved down and forward, accepting every forceful movement.

"Eli. You feel so good," I moaned.

He'd overwhelmed me, just like I'd always wished he would, but I hadn't been prepared for just how amazing it was.

I'd never felt more alive. Every cell in my body was filled with the taste, smell, and feel of Eli Stone.

It was too much.

Yet it wasn't enough.

"Take what you need, Jade," Eli said roughly. "I'm not going to last."

I went with my instinct since I had no idea what I needed. I tightened my legs around him, keeping his thrusts short and fast. It was exactly what I needed to get some stimulation to my clit.

My climax rose up to meet me ferociously, and it was almost scary.

"Eli," I moaned as I felt every muscle in my body tense.

The pressure was nearly unbearable until the hot wave of pleasure washed over me, hitting me so hard that my body started to shake. I rode that wave of pleasure as it took me over and then spit me back out again.

I felt Eli's muscles contract, and I knew the clench and release of my internal muscles had milked him to climax.

"Fuck!" he cursed fiercely, his breath ragged and erratic.

I panted for air as we both tried to catch our breath.

Eli hefted my body up a little higher, walked to the couch, and collapsed down onto it. He landed on his back and cushioned my fall with his body.

Our bodies were slick with sweat, and I waited silently for my heart and respirations to return to normal.

"That was incredible," I told Eli when I'd finally come back into my body.

"There's only one problem," he answered in a lazy voice.

I moved back so I could see his face. "What problem?"

I couldn't find a single thing wrong with what had just occurred.

He cocked an eyebrow. "I still haven't managed to get you into my bed."

"You haven't asked me," I teased.

He sat up, cradling my body as he stood. "I'm not asking. I'm just going to take you there. I refuse to give you the chance to say no."

I smiled against his shoulder. Eli had never been good at asking for anything, but in our current situation, I was willing to let him be as high-handed as he wanted to be.

CHAPTER 24

ELI

"Holy fuck!" I cursed, angry because I couldn't seem to control my own body.

I shrugged out of my suit coat as I stumbled forward, my body hitting my bed with a giant *thud!*

"Son of a bitch!" I rasped, my throat so sore that I could barely get the words out of my mouth.

Maybe I *was* a billionaire mogul, but right now I couldn't put two coherent sentences together.

I rolled over onto my stomach, and was immediately hit by Jade's tantalizing scent that still lingered on the pillow from the night before.

Butterfly.

She'd left my place earlier in the day, after I'd gone into the office, but her seductive fragrance was still with me.

As sick as I was at the moment, my body still reacted immediately to the smell of her on my sheets.

I need to call her. I shouldn't have left without talking to her this morning.

As I'd watched her sleep like an angel, exhausted from getting very little sleep during the night, my heart hadn't allowed me to wake her up, even though I knew we needed to talk. So I'd gone into the office to catch everything up so we could spend more time together and talk about everything we should have discussed a long time ago.

Jade was mine, and I sure as hell knew I was hers. If I wanted to get real, I'd known it almost from the first minute we'd met. My Butterfly had grabbed my balls and my heart from day one. I'd just been having a very hard time accepting that I deserved a woman like her, and that she'd be stuck with me for life if I acted on those emotions.

But I was done fucking fighting my fate. I'd never wanted to in the first place. My only real apprehension had been saddling a woman like her with a guy like me, so I'd found every excuse possible *not* to do it.

Truth was, I'd been a major dick, and it had taken some kind of come-to-Jesus moment like I'd experienced last night to snap me back into reality.

I needed her, and I just hoped to hell she felt the same way. Screw the fact that I didn't deserve her. I'd make her so damn happy that she'd never regret taking me on.

I fumbled for my cell phone in my pocket.

She *needed* to know how I felt.

I *wanted* her to know.

But the synapses in my brain weren't quite connecting all that well, and the flu medication I'd taken didn't seem to be helping much. One moment I was burning hot, and the next I was cold to the bone.

Just the exertion of reaching for my cell phone had me hacking and coughing so hard that my ribs ached.

Need to call Jade.

But I don't want her to come here, because I'm currently contaminating my entire home.

Not sure I could even hold a conversation at the moment, much less tell Jade everything I wanted to say, I tried to focus on my phone, and just texted exactly what I was feeling. Then I dropped the cell on the bed, my energy spent just from typing some words into a text.

I rolled over onto my back with a groan. My entire body felt like it was on fire, and I hurt from the top of the head to my damn toes.

All I wanted was to escape being miserable, and I got my wish when the medication I'd taken finally kicked in and I fell into a restless sleep.

⌁

"She still hasn't answered?" I asked my mom in a hoarse voice as I lay in a hospital bed seven days after I'd initially gotten sick, my body being pumped with fluids because I was dehydrated.

As if the flu hadn't been bad enough, I'd ended up getting a secondary bacterial pneumonia that had delivered the knockout punch. My damn cough had gotten so bad that my chest and my ribs felt like I'd been slugged repeatedly with a baseball bat in those areas.

My mother glanced at my phone and said, "I don't see any new text messages."

"Shit! What if I got Jade sick, too? She was with me the night before I left the office because I was coming down with the flu. Maybe something happened to her."

"She's fine, Eli," my mother said as she ran a gentle hand over my sweaty forehead. "She just texted me yesterday to ask a question about one of her investments. She's not sick."

Jesus! I felt like a kid again with my mother keeping watch at my bedside. And I hated it. I was a grown man, and it was deflating to be so damn weak that my mom had to help out.

"So she isn't pissed or angry at *you*," I confirmed. "She just isn't talking to *me*."

That hurt like a bitch. I was sure I'd let Jade know that I didn't want her to rush to San Diego for me because I was sick. In fact, I'd been trying to make certain she didn't, because I hadn't wanted to infect her. But she could have at least answered my texts.

Something.

Anything.

Although I was glad that she wasn't ill, I desperately needed some kind of communication from her. I'd been on her list of people to ignore once before, and I hadn't liked it.

Because I felt like I was constantly hacking up a lung, I probably couldn't talk. But I could text.

Sort of.

My mother gave me a suspicious look. "Why would she be angry at you?"

"No reason," I muttered, wishing I hadn't said anything to her.

My mother could be like a hunting dog on the fresh scent of game when she wanted to be. She'd chase down an answer if it killed her.

I started to cough again, and the pain that shot through my ribs felt like somebody was nailing me with a hot knife. "I hate being sick," I grumbled irritably as soon as my body had calmed down.

My mother smiled. "You've always been a bad patient. Luckily, you don't get ill very often."

I was relieved that she didn't seem ready to hound me about Jade.

"I have your pain medication, Mr. Stone," a friendly nurse said as she breezed into the room.

"I don't want pain medication," I said like a petulant kid. "It screws with my head."

I'd just woken up from the previous dose. The last thing I needed was to conk out again.

The nurse looked at me disapprovingly. "If you don't keep your pain level down, you won't be able to do the deep breathing and coughing like you need to do. That means the pneumonia could get worse than it is right now."

I weighed my choices with a frown, and then took the pill cup from her hand, tossed back the medication, and swallowed it with some water.

If I had to be out of it for days, so be it.

Since Jade wasn't answering me, I was determined to go and find her the moment I was able to get the hell out of bed.

And taking any longer than absolutely necessary to get healthy again was *not* an option.

CHAPTER 25

Jade

"It's been nearly two weeks, Brooke. I don't think Eli is going to call."

My words hung in the air like a dark cloud as I chatted on the phone with my sister.

I looked down at the text messages that I'd received from Eli the day after we'd slept together. I'd probably stared at them a thousand times, but they still didn't make any sense. But the message was loud and clear.

Don't want to see you.
Don't want you here with me.
Better off being alone.

There was really no question about what he'd been thinking after we'd slept together.

He was done with our relationship, and his swift rejection had nearly broken me.

Okay, I'd *rationally* known that there was a chance that things might not turn out well between me and Eli, but I hadn't expected that the night he'd finally taken me to his bed would be the last time I ever saw him.

We'd reached for each other all night long, both of us hungry for the passion that we found every time we touched.

To be honest, we hadn't really *slept* much, so I hadn't expected to wake up to find Eli already gone to his office in the morning. His driver had arrived to take me home during the late morning, but I hadn't really been worried. It was the radio silence I'd had from him for fourteen straight days after his text messages that told me that he didn't ever intend to see me again.

"Honestly, Jade, I just don't see it," Brooke answered. "I don't know what's up with the weird text messages, but the guy is crazy about you."

"Maybe he wasn't," I said thoughtfully. "Maybe I was just a distraction."

I hadn't uttered a word about the things that Eli had told me the last time I saw him. It was personal, and I was pretty sure that he hadn't shared the experience with very many people.

My heart still bled for him, even though we hadn't seen each other. Not only had he lost his twin brother, but his father had died two years after Austin. So while he was still trying to twist himself into a person he was not, he'd had to give up his own dreams to take over for his dad.

How does anyone recover from two enormous losses so close together in their life?

"You were not a *distraction*," Brooke answered. "Nobody acts like he did when you were in the hospital, over a casual fling. He has feelings for you, Jade. I can't say that I understand what happened, but I'm positive I'm right. I think it's more likely that he's afraid of the way he feels, and wants to run away."

"It doesn't matter," I muttered as I got my lazy butt off the couch and headed to the kitchen. "Whatever the reason, I'm not going to see him anymore. I wish it had lasted longer, but I *knew* what I was getting myself into when I started seeing him. No commitments. No strings attached. It was just sex."

Really, really good sex.

"You can't fool me, Jade. Please don't try to sound philosophical. It's not working. He broke your heart."

"He did," I admitted softly. "But I'll get over it. I'll have to."

I'd been crying nonstop for the last two weeks, and it needed to stop. Even if Eli was running away, I couldn't stop him from doing it.

"Oh, Jade. I'm so sorry. He's such a jerk for hurting you."

"I thought you liked him," I reminded her.

"I did. But I don't anymore," she said adamantly. "How could I still like him if he doesn't have enough sense to know what he had?"

I sighed. That was one thing in my family that was always consistent: if you mess with one Sinclair, you're messing with them all. We all stood by each other no matter what.

"Please don't say anything to our brothers," I requested. "You know how they are."

"I'm not so sure that I don't want to see them clean Eli's clock," Brooke said.

"Brooke," I said in a warning voice.

"Oh, all right. I won't say a word," she promised, sounding like staying quiet was the last thing she wanted to do.

"I'll be okay, Brooke," I said, not sure if I was trying to reassure my twin or myself.

"I know you will," she replied softly. "I just hate seeing you hurting now."

"Sometimes experiencing pain leads to something good, right? Look what you went through. And you found Liam because of it."

Brooke snorted. "You've been reading too many romance books, sister. Pain sucks. And don't let anybody tell you otherwise. But I did find Liam."

"Okay. If you want to know the truth, I've been thinking about calling him. I have to fight my instincts every damn day. And it does hurt."

"I know," Brooke said with a sigh. "I can feel your pain."

I had no idea why I ever tried to brush things off when I talked to Brooke. Maybe because she was so happy, and I didn't want to be a downer. But she always knew, just like I could always tell when something was wrong with her.

My twin and I had the same kind of connection that I knew Eli had experienced with his brother.

"He's gone through a lot, Brooke. I can't tell you everything, but he went through something terrible. So maybe he is running away. I know he cared about me."

"I know he did, too," she agreed. "Look, maybe you should talk to him. It was pretty damn clear that he really cared about you, Jade. And I wouldn't ever get your hopes up if I didn't believe it."

"I think Eli and I are actually a lot alike," I mused. "I found out he was a science geek, too. He has a PhD in aerospace engineering, Brooke. He went to Caltech."

"Holy crap!" she exclaimed. "Do you have any idea how selective they are?"

"I know. And his money didn't get him in there. He's probably smarter than I am."

"But I don't understand why he isn't working in the field," Brooke commented.

"His dad's death was unexpected," I explained, trying not to lie to my sister. "He took over after his father passed away."

"Is he okay with that?"

I thought about her question before I answered. "I'm not sure. But he does have his own aerospace lab, so it isn't like he isn't still involved in rocketry."

"Talk to him, Jade."

I paused before I said, "He did offer to make me his unofficial intern so I could learn about conglomerates and investing."

"Perfect," she said happily.

"And I suppose it's time for a makeover," I added. "And a whole new wardrobe."

"Don't change who you are for him, Jade," she cautioned.

"I'm not a student anymore, Brooke. I have a PhD. If I'm eventually going to get into any kind of management or professional career, I'm going to have to learn how to dress the part."

"If you want that, then do it. You're right. I had to dress up to work in the bank every day. I didn't love it at first, but I kind of miss it now."

"Maybe because you have a lot more funds to buy new clothes these days," I teased. "Did you decide what you're going to do in Amesport?"

I knew damn well my sister would never be happy not working.

"I can't go back to a bank," she shared. "The memories are too painful. But I'm starting to look at my other options."

"You'll be outstanding no matter what you decide to do," I told her. "And you're not exactly hard up for funds. You can take your time."

Brooke had been through enough emotional trauma.

"Liam keeps me busy," she joked. "And it's kind of fun to do analysis on possible investments. That might be where I end up someday."

Brooke was happy whenever she was knee-deep in numbers. "Then maybe you can manage my money, too," I said hopefully.

"I'm entirely certain you can do that yourself," she answered confidently. "Especially when you'll be learning from Eli. He really has an uncanny ability to see the big picture on his investments. He's taken over some corporations that should have been impossible to recover. But he manages to turn them into profit monsters after he changes the direction of the company."

"Showing up at his office won't be easy," I mumbled.

"You're the gutsiest person I know," Brooke replied. "And you're brilliant. But you've spent most of your adult life in school and studying.

You just haven't really had a chance to function in the business world yet. But I have no doubt you'll do fantastic."

"I'm still applying for a lot of positions," I told her. "But I still have no idea where I'll end up."

"I know you want to do long-term research. And you're plenty qualified."

"I'm more than willing to start in an entry position," I explained. "But I really want to be a permanent part of a team. There's so much happening in genetic conservation now, and most of the groundbreaking stuff is going to take decades to build on."

"Are you applying for anything on the East Coast?" she asked hopefully.

"I'm pretty much applying for positions without consideration to geography. I can live anywhere."

"Fingers crossed for something closer to me," Brooke teased.

"I'll keep you posted," I replied.

"First things first," she said. "Go find a dynamite business wardrobe that has a little bit of sexy. I can't wait to see you turn Eli inside out."

I was fairly certain that Eli Stone was already tormented, and it had nothing to do with me, but I didn't mention it.

We chatted for a few more minutes about the family, and then we hung up.

I was on the computer moments later trying to figure out who I could hire to make a science geek into a professional.

Turns out, it wasn't all that hard.

CHAPTER 26

ELI

Don't want to see you.
Don't want you here with me.
Better off being alone.

I stared at my text messages for the hundredth time in the last hour, and wondered what in the fuck I'd been thinking.

Granted, my brain had been fried from my illness at the time, but could I have done anything more stupid than send Jade asinine messages like the ones I was staring at?

Nope. Probably not.

What I'd *thought* I'd said, and what *I'd really typed* couldn't have been more different. Yeah, I hadn't wanted her to come to San Diego because I was afraid she'd end up sick, too. Actually, I'd desperately wanted to *see her*, and I'd wanted her to *be with me*. But I'd preferred *to be alone* because of the contagious nature of my initial illness.

I'd been so fucked up that I'd *felt* like I'd poured my heart out to her. But in reality, I'd pretty much dumped her via text message.

Shit!

I tossed my phone on my desk with more force than was really necessary because I was disgusted with myself.

I should have looked at what I'd texted to her earlier, but it hadn't occurred to me that I'd sent something that idiotic to the woman I couldn't live without. Besides, I hadn't wanted to look at the unanswered messages. It would have made me even more miserable than I'd already been when I was really sick.

I was going to do what I absolutely had to do in my office, and then I was driving my Bugatti to Citrus Beach to see Jade in person as fast as I could haul ass to get there.

No more text messages.

No phone calls that she could easily ignore like she had in the past when she'd been angry.

Now that I was finally lucid, I planned on getting it right. And that might involve groveling until I could get Jade to let me explain the jumbled messages I'd just discovered an hour ago.

"And I wondered why she wasn't calling me?" I said aloud in my empty office.

Hell, she had to think I was even a bigger prick than she'd first thought.

We'd slept together.

And then I'd sent her a rambling message that sounded more like I didn't want her than its true intention—to tell her how I actually felt.

I would have been better off to leave my phone alone while my mind had been messed up when I was sick. But I was so damn obsessed with Jade that even when I was barely coherent, all I'd thought about was trying to explain everything to her.

I looked at the files and papers that had piled up in my absence.

The only things I planned on taking care of before I left for Citrus Beach were anything urgent or time sensitive. Then I was getting the hell out of the office so I could take all the time I needed to convince Jade that we needed to be together.

Not for ten days.

Not until our passion faded—which was never going to happen.

Not as friends—because I'd never survive just a friendship.

I was getting *forever*. And I'd camp out in Citrus Beach until she agreed.

"Jade Sinclair to see you, Mr. Stone." Alice's voice rang out from the intercom, her tone professional.

Jade?

Damned if my heart didn't start to accelerate just from knowing she was standing outside my office.

I looked up from the papers I was signing, my mind suddenly on alert. Unfortunately, my dick was suddenly at attention, too. All it took was to hear *her* name.

Not that I could exactly do anything about *that* right now. But it was good to know that everything was still functioning after over two weeks of misery.

It had been seventeen days, five hours, and a handful of minutes since I'd seen Jade. I felt every single second of not hearing her voice or seeing her beautiful face.

Today had been the first day I'd felt reasonably human again, and I'd known from the moment I'd gotten out of bed that I couldn't go another day without talking to Jade.

Yeah, the doctor had told me it would take some time until I felt back up to my normal speed after the drain of having bacterial pneumonia. But I'd been on antibiotics long enough to be certain I wasn't contagious anymore. It hadn't mattered that I was still dragging ass. I knew I was going to see Jade or die trying.

But she's here now.

And holy fuck . . . I *needed* to see her.

I was irritated as hell about being sick. I hadn't gotten the flu since I was a kid, and it had been the last thing my relationship with Jade had needed.

I pressed the intercom button. "Give me a minute, Alice," I instructed my secretary.

"Let me know when you're ready, Mr. Stone," she replied.

I stood up and walked to the bathroom, splashed some water on my face, and then stared at my reflection.

At some point over the last few weeks, I'd finally figured out that I didn't need to be Austin. My brother would always have a place in my memory, but he died because he had an addiction problem. Nobody could cure him when he hadn't wanted to be sober himself. We'd all tried. My parents had done everything they could to get him straightened out, and I'd pretty much begged him to stop. But the will had needed to come from him, and he'd never made the effort to stay clean. Not really. He'd gone to rehab to satisfy my parents and not himself.

Only after I'd lost it with Jade had I been able to actually evaluate the emotions that hadn't seen the light of day in four years.

And I wasn't very happy with the way I'd handled Austin's death.

I also wasn't pleased at the fact that I'd been offered the chance to be with an amazing woman like Jade, and I'd pretty much pissed away the opportunity because I'd been a dick.

I'd known that Jade was special from the moment we met.

I should have been pursuing a real relationship.

Instead, I'd thought that all I needed was sex.

Yeah, maybe I *did* need it with her pretty damn bad, but I wanted a hell of a lot more than just Jade's body.

I fucking wanted her heart.

I'd just been too damn slow to realize that.

Now, it was very likely that I'd pay for that stupid mistake.

But I'm not going to lose her. It doesn't matter what it takes to make sure she ends up with me.

I tossed the towel I'd used to dry my face into the hamper.

Moment of truth, Stone.

It was about damn time that I fought for exactly what I wanted, and the only thing I really needed was the woman who was waiting outside my office.

I sat back down in my chair and took a deep breath before I pressed the intercom. "Send her in, Alice," I instructed.

"Right away, sir," she answered immediately.

I shook my head, wondering if the secretary who had been with me for several years now was ever going to call me Eli like I'd asked her to about a million times before.

The errant thought left my mind as Alice appeared, and Jade came strolling through the door.

I knew the moment that she directly met my eyes that something was way different.

It took a couple of seconds for all the changes to completely sink in.

I didn't notice the soft click of the door closing that signaled Alice had left us alone. I was too busy watching the woman who had walked into my office like she owned it.

There was no hesitation, no nervous new female billionaire like I'd encountered the last time she entered my office.

Her beautiful eyes were wide open and taking my measure as she walked up to the desk.

Jesus Christ! What in the hell happened to the Jade I knew?

Gone were her blue jeans and T-shirt, and in their place was a figure-hugging, black leather pencil skirt that ended above her knees, making her legs seem to go on forever. As far as attire went, she was pretty much dressed for business, but her white blouse was cut just a little too low. And the short cashmere sweater that she was wearing open over the top of the silky creation that had my attention sure as hell wasn't made to keep her warm.

She moved gracefully in a pair of black heels, and as she arrived in front of my desk, she dropped the stylish black purse into the chair next to the one she sat down in.

"What did you do to your hair?" I rasped.

The locks were pulled to one side with an enormous clip, and cascaded down one shoulder. But it wasn't the style that had thrown me. It was the color.

Jade was a brunette, but her hair was more of an auburn shade now, the red highlights likely to make any guy do a double take. I didn't like it, but my eager dick certainly did.

"It's new," she said vaguely. "I guess I needed a change."

A change?

Buying a new pair of shoes was *a change.*

Everything about Jade seemed entirely different right now, including the makeup she didn't generally wear.

"You look beautiful," I said in a husky voice.

There had never been a day when Jade hadn't been the most attractive woman I'd ever seen, but she looked particularly stunning today.

She shrugged, but kept her eyes locked with mine. "Thank you," she said breezily. "But I'm not here for compliments. I'm taking you up on the offer to be your intern if it's still open."

"Of course it is," I said eagerly. "But Jade, I wanted to talk about—"

She put her hand up. "You don't need to explain. I just want a chance to learn. I'm not asking for anything else."

I wanted her to ask for anything she damn well wanted. I'd find a way to give it to her.

"I'm sorry that I—"

I immediately got another "talk to the hand" motion. "I don't need an apology for anything. We had a good time, Eli. Now it's time for me to get down to business."

She's not going to accept my apology. She's not going to listen because she isn't interested in a prick like me.

Not that I could really blame her. Looking back now, I knew I'd been a complete asshole. She might have been looking for a real relationship had I not told her that basically all I wanted was sex.

"I was just looking at a new potential investment," I told her. "It's a pretty big one, so I have a lot of analysis to do."

In truth, I hadn't been looking at shit. I'd been scribbling my signature on papers that had to get signed before I left to go track her beautiful ass down. But I did have proposals on my desk, and one in particular that was a big project that needed more research.

There wasn't much I wouldn't do to at least keep her within my sight. So I'd roll with the intern thing for now. I wanted to understand what was really happening with her, and I was willing to take all the time in the world to figure it out.

"Good," she said cheerfully as she rose and started to scoot her chair around the desk. "Can I look with you?"

She shoved her chair against mine and sat back down.

Being a red-blooded male who had never been able to keep my eyes off her in the first place, I couldn't help being fixated on her legs as she crossed them, and that tight skirt that was riding up her thighs.

I caught a whiff of a light, clean, floral scent that made my dick turn into stone.

She's killing me, but at least I'll die pretty fucking happy.

I tore my eyes away from her and turned back to the computer screen.

"Show me what you're doing?" she requested.

I spent the next few hours torn between happiness and agony.

There was nothing I wanted more than just to be next to her.

But every time she got up to get something, go to the restroom, or just to stretch, my eyes and my dick were drawn to that little leather skirt.

And dammit, she seemed so happy and confident. The real bitch in that was the fact that she'd done it all *without me*.

However, I had to marvel over the quickness of her brain, and how fast she caught on to the concerns that come with any investment. Her questions came like lightning, and she seemed to absorb everything I said and then build on that knowledge.

"So what's your final decision?" she asked curiously as we finished up reviewing the information.

"I need to order a couple more reports," I explained. "But it looks good so far. It will be a challenge. But if I can save jobs for the employees, it might be worth it."

"Do you think you can save the company if you acquire it?"

"I'm reasonably sure I can, but there's going to have to be changes company-wide. And sometimes people don't like change. I figured that out a long time ago."

"It's not always a bad thing," she said thoughtfully.

I heard the intercom beep, and Alice's voice floated into the room. "I'm going for lunch, Mr. Stone. Can I bring you anything?"

"I'm good," I told her.

"You really should eat something, sir," Alice said carefully. "Those antibiotics will make you sick if you don't."

"I'm fine, Alice. Go to lunch," I replied firmly.

I had a few more days on my antibiotics, but the course was almost done.

"Back in an hour," she said.

"Are you sick, Eli?" Jade asked quietly.

I could hear the concern in her voice, and it was the first time I had a glimpse of the Jade I cared about. "It's nothing. Are you hungry?"

She stood, put her hand on her shapely hip, and drilled me with a no-nonsense look. "Eli Stone, why are you taking antibiotics? Are you ill?"

"I'm not contagious," I confessed. "But I had a fight with the flu and pneumonia. The viruses and bacteria won."

She held out her hand, and I took it because she was so damn fierce that I didn't even consider refusing.

"I'm taking you to lunch," she informed me as I got to my feet. "And then you'll explain why you're even back in the office if you aren't fully recovered."

She grabbed her purse on the way to the door, but tightened her hold on my hand. "What sounds good?" she questioned as we left the office together.

"Nothing," I said honestly.

"Good. Then soup and sandwiches it is," she decided.

I grinned as we waited for her vehicle to be brought around by the valet. She'd gotten decidedly bossy, but I kind of liked it. Jade had always been meant to lead instead of be hidden away in the woods somewhere. She'd just never realized that she was fully capable of doing more than one thing, or being good at a whole lot of things.

I'd never doubted it.

"This is me," she said, pointing toward an arriving vehicle.

"Since when are you driving a BMW?" I asked in surprise. "What happened to the Jeep?"

"I still have it," she answered as she moved to the driver's side and handed the valet a tip. "I need it for my survival stuff. But I think it was time to buy a new vehicle. It's not exactly a Bugatti, but I love it."

I headed for the passenger's side. It was a 3 series, so it wasn't an extravagant spend for her, but the classy black exterior suited her.

"And the butterfly finally escapes from the cocoon, stretches her wings, and flies away," I muttered as I got into the car.

Jade had indeed broken out of the protective shell she'd lived in, but she wasn't escaping very far.

If I had my way—which I would—she was flying home to me.

CHAPTER 27

JADE

I'd been in Eli's office early every single day for the last two weeks.

Maybe I'd planned to try to be businesslike, and for the most part, I'd succeeded. But I'd nearly crumbled that first day when I'd found out that he'd been sick enough to end up in the hospital.

In my heart of hearts, maybe I really wanted to believe that Eli hadn't called me because he'd been too sick to do so. And the excuse was likely plausible, since he'd personally told me that much of what had happened during his illness was a blur. He'd been on a ton of medication, including pain meds, during his hospitalization.

But then . . . there were those heartbreaking texts. I hadn't asked about them. Perhaps I honestly didn't want to know.

For the most part, we talked about business, and that seemed to be enough for him. So I'd just continued to be his makeshift intern, harboring some stupid idea that he hadn't called me because he'd been physically incapacitated.

Had I looked closely when I'd first seen him in the office, I would have noticed that he had lost some weight, and he hadn't had the energy he usually did. But I'd been so busy worrying about him finding out that I was a fraud that I hadn't been *really looking* at him.

Once I had discovered that he'd been in the hospital, he hadn't looked so good.

I brought breakfast every morning, and made sure he ate lunch. As the days passed, we frequented better and better restaurants, most of them his eateries, for lunch.

He was fully recovered now, and probably had been for at least a week. But I still found myself looking forward to seeing him every single morning.

Our days were productive, and I'd gotten to the point where I could preview some of the proposals he had stacked up on his desk. If they were definitely duds, I could save him time by pointing out why they weren't going to work, and I could toss him the ones that were questionable.

All in all, I was learning fast and getting more comfortable in my business suits. Well, maybe I wasn't *literally* used to my wardrobe, but I was starting to feel more like a businesswoman.

"Good morning, Alice," I said happily as I came through the door to the outer offices.

The gray-haired woman smiled. "Good morning, Ms. Sinclair."

"Cheese omelet with a bagel, cream cheese on the side," I informed her as I put the boxed breakfast on her desk. "And when are you going to call me Jade?"

Alice and I had struck up a friendship while I'd been working with Eli, but I still hadn't been able to get her to stop being so formal.

"Probably about the same time that I refer to Mr. Stone by his first name. It's been years, so stop trying to teach an old woman new tricks," she advised.

I laughed, and picked up one of the many magazines on her desk. "What's all this?"

"New magazines," she answered. "It was the strangest thing. Mr. Stone asked me to change our subscriptions right after your first visit here."

I rummaged through the magazines, trying not to mess them up.

Time.

Rolling Stone.

National Geographic.

Wired.

The Economist.

The Atlantic.

Harper's.

There wasn't one single fluffy women's magazine in the bunch. "Oh, my God." I let out a silly giggle that I'd never heard come from my lips before. I couldn't believe that Eli had actually taken my advice on reading material in his waiting room.

"What's the matter?" Alice asked.

"Not a thing," I answered with a smile on my face. "Is Eli already in?"

She nodded. "He just got in a few minutes ago."

I juggled my boxes and moved forward, not arguing when Alice got up to open his office door for me.

"Good morning," I said to Eli as I carried the boxes to his desk.

"You could have called me down to help you," he grumbled as he stood up. "And it is a good morning now."

Just like I'd been doing for the last two weeks, I pretty much ignored his compliment, and wondered how much longer I could play the good intern.

I'd put myself in a dangerous situation by accepting the relationship. But I wasn't sure if I could keep pretending that I wasn't crazy in love with the CEO.

Eli had retreated to wash his hands, and I took the food out of its protective container.

I bent and stretched across the desk to put Eli's stuff on his side of the desk.

I squeaked as a strong body slammed into me from the back. Eli covered my hands with his, his front plastered against my back as he growled, "If you bend over my desk one more fucking time, I'm not responsible for what happens after that."

I closed my eyes and took a deep breath. Unfortunately, all I could smell was Eli's masculine scent.

"Does it bother you?" I asked.

I wasn't about to shy away from him. My whole objective had been to get him to notice me and realize that he cared. Lately, I'd come to the conclusion that I was just like one of the pathetic women in the magazines who wants to catch a man she can't have, and who doesn't want her.

"Hell, yes, it bothers me," he said in a husky voice next to my ear. "*You* bother me, Butterfly. Do you know how damn hard it's been not to bend you over my desk and make my dick happier than it's ever been? You have the most gorgeous ass I've ever seen."

Everything inside me wanted to give in, but as I contemplated how I'd feel later if I let him fuck me, my stomach got tied up in knots.

I wanted him desperately.

But I knew I deserved more.

"Let go," I requested as I pushed back against his chest. "I don't want this, Eli."

He backed away immediately.

"I can't do this anymore," I told him as I turned to get my purse. "I have to go."

Even though my heart was breaking, I knew I needed to finally find the strength to walk away.

It wasn't fair to ask him to change, and I'd known the arrangement going in . . . sex only, with no commitments.

It wasn't his fault that I needed more.

"Jade, wait. We need to talk. Listen to me—"

"No," I interrupted. "*You* listen to *me*."

I was done playing games. But I wasn't leaving until he heard everything I needed to say. "I played your silly cat-and-mouse game in the beginning because I wanted to get to know you. I have no problem admitting that I also wanted to end up in your bed because I was so damn attracted to you. But I ran into a problem somewhere along the way." I took a deep breath and looked at him as I continued. "I ended up wanting more, Eli. Even though you made it pretty clear that you didn't. This isn't really your fault. You were honest. It was *me* who fell in love with *you*. I didn't want to, but it happened. I should have gotten the message when I didn't hear from you after we slept together. And it *definitely* should have sunk in when you texted me about how you felt. But I wasn't sure if you needed time to sort through everything that happened with your brother. Or if you didn't call me because you were so sick. I foolishly thought that you might eventually realize that you loved me, too. But you didn't. So I *have* to move on. Empty sex isn't going to ever be enough for me. I'm not made that way. I'm sorry."

"It was never empty, Jade," I heard him say as I moved like lightning toward the door.

I didn't answer. I couldn't. I had to leave before I ended up making a bigger fool out of myself.

I pulled out my cell phone as I moved down the hallway as fast as my high-heeled shoes would take me.

"Huge tip if you get my BMW to the front door before I get down the elevator and outside," I said to the valet on my cell.

"I'm on it," the valet answered.

I jumped into an open lift and pushed the button for the lobby, thankful that nobody else had entered the same one.

I let my head fall back as I rode down, trying unsuccessfully to hold back the tears that desperately wanted to escape from my eyes.

"You can do this, Jade. You can do this," I whispered to myself.

Maybe I would have lasted another week if Eli hadn't touched me. But what good would it have done? I couldn't make him love me, and

I loved him so much that I couldn't take the pain of being close to him every single day and not want more.

When the elevator opened, I strode across the marble floors, my heels clicking wildly as I made my way outside.

My BMW was just pulling up to the curb.

"Hey, Mr. Stone said to hold up," a second valet called from near the building.

The guy who jumped out of my car hesitated, but I pushed several twenties into his hand as I said, "Mr. Stone doesn't always get everything he wants."

I hopped into my car and left, and I finally had the very ugly cry I'd been holding back. It lasted all the way to Citrus Beach.

CHAPTER 28

Jade

I found out later that day that I had gotten an interview for my dream job as a researcher/scientist in San Diego, so I knew I had to pull my shit back together.

It was Friday, and I had to be coherent by Monday.

Maybe I should have called Skye or Brooke, but I didn't want to do much of anything except lie on my couch and devour as much ice cream as possible.

My food drug of choice was Stephen Colbert's AmeriCone Dream that was made by Ben & Jerry's. And I was well stocked. Besides the carton I had in my hand, there were four more in the freezer.

I dug my spoon into the caramel and chocolate-covered-ice-cream-cone mixture and shoved it into my mouth before I picked up the remote and started flipping through the channels.

Yeah, I realized that I couldn't sit and eat Ben & Jerry's every night, but I needed some time to get my head together.

Maybe approaching Eli to follow through on his offer to act as an intern hadn't been a good idea, but I didn't regret it. I'd learned a lot, and those few weeks had helped me gain some confidence in a world I knew nothing about.

I also didn't regret the new wardrobe. I'd need it if I was going to start interviewing.

The makeover had boosted my confidence, and I finally felt okay in my own skin.

I was over my guilt about becoming a billionaire. I was more interested in figuring out how I could make a difference with my wealth.

At some point over the last several weeks, I'd changed. I'd stopped being the shy student, and had decided to be the best person I could be.

Eli had helped me get there, so I didn't regret the time I'd spent with him.

What I really felt devastated over was the fact that Eli hadn't returned my feelings, and I wasn't so sure I was ever going to feel the same way about a man again.

I stopped changing channels when I got to *Shark Tank*, and tossed the remote back on the coffee table. I could listen to the show while I was answering my emails.

I opened my laptop and started deleting all the junk mail I got on a daily basis. It seemed like I unsubscribed from a million places, but I still had more ads in my box the next day.

I clicked on a notice from the DNA site I'd used when I'd discovered that Evan was my half brother. I went to delete it because I got ads or notifications almost every day, but I hesitated when I saw the first line.

I have a new match?

I clicked to the site and looked at the current entry. I scanned with a little more interest when I saw that I had a new *relative match*.

Relationship—Niece.

"What the hell?" I mumbled. "How is that possible?"

I was a scientist. And DNA didn't lie.

My mind raced as I stared at the notification. There was no *half* designation, so the logical conclusion was that one of my brothers had fathered a child. But none of them were old enough to have a grown daughter.

"It wasn't Brooke," I said aloud. "It *has* to be one of my brothers."

I couldn't imagine any of my siblings walking away from their own daughter, but there was a possibility they'd never known that they had impregnated a woman they had dated. None of my brothers had lacked female attention, and they'd all had girlfriends. But the whole thing wasn't sitting right with me.

How could they not know?

And which one of them had a child they didn't know existed?

There was no real information about who my niece might be, but I could write to the relative through the site.

I wrote a few lines, introducing myself and letting them know that they'd matched to me.

I still had to wonder if the information was somehow incorrect.

I'd just reached for my cell to call Brooke when the doorbell rang. *Probably Aiden or Seth.*

I got my rear off the couch and headed toward the door. I wasn't exactly dressed for visitors, but it wasn't like my brothers hadn't seen me in my pajama shorts and a sweatshirt before.

I opened the door, startled at first because no one was standing there.

Then I heard a yelp of excitement.

"Charlie?" I opened the screen door and let the canine in, and then reached down to pet him. "What are you doing here?"

I frowned as I noticed something attached to his collar.

There was an envelope that said *Read me first* and a small box that said *Keep me.*

Both were lightly attached, so I pulled them off Charlie's collar, sat down on the floor to cuddle with the canine I'd come to adore, and opened the envelope.

If Charlie is here, I know Eli isn't very far away.

My heart stuttered at the thought that Eli was probably close by. What was he up to?

The big, gaping wound I'd opened when I'd confronted Eli this morning was still raw, and I wasn't sure I could bear to see him so soon.

I pulled out the papers that were in the envelope, my hands shaking with emotion.

"Oh, Eli, what did you do?" I whispered as I looked at the quit-claim deed.

He'd deeded the Lucifer's Canyon property to me.

I dropped the paper in my lap and wrapped my arms around Charlie as tears flowed down my cheeks.

I was pretty sure it meant that the property didn't have a hold on Eli anymore. And if he was finally free of his demons, I was happy for him.

"It's really hell when I have to be jealous of my mutt," I heard Eli's baritone say hoarsely from the door.

I got up, and picked up the box and the deed. "What are you doing here? And why did you do this?" I motioned to the paper.

He opened the screen door and stepped in. "Because I want you to have it. There's no strings attached, no matter what you say about what's in the box."

"I haven't opened it yet."

"Don't," he requested. "Not yet."

He took my hand and led me into the small living room. I grabbed the remote and turned off the TV. "I was just . . . eating," I said as I grabbed the container of ice cream, took it to the kitchen, and tossed it in the freezer. Since it was a tiny house, I was back in seconds.

I stopped in front of him, my chest aching because he looked so damn good in a pair of jeans and a sweater. "Eli, I—"

He put his fingers on my lips. "No. Don't talk. I have some things I want to say before you run away again."

I nodded, and he started to use his thumb to wipe the tears from my face.

"I want to thank you for helping me get my head straight. I buried everything about my brother for way too long. So long that I guess I wasn't sure what was me and what was Austin anymore. Because of you, I think I have everything figured out now."

"So what was you?" I asked.

"When I started doing the things Austin did, I did it on my own terms. He did crazy things just because he wanted to do them. I did them to make money for my charities. So I guess some of it was always me. And there are a few things I actually do like to do for me, like the mountain climbing and the car racing. But I can do without the useless things. So I'll do what I want and dump the others. I don't have a death wish like Austin did."

"And the tats?"

"Done to honor my brother. I don't regret it."

I didn't think he needed to be remorseful about anything, but I didn't speak because I wanted him to keep talking.

He added, "I framed all the pictures that Joel gave me. I realized that I can't keep hating him for what my brother did to himself. My mother said that Joel cleaned up his act after Austin died, so one good thing came out of my brother's death. And I think it's time for me to remember the good things about my twin and not try to completely forget the past."

"Do you regret that you gave up your own dreams to take over your dad's interests?" I asked.

He shook his head slowly. "I don't. It turns out that I can do both. I'm pretty involved in my aerospace company, and there's a certain satisfaction in taking over companies and making them better than they were before."

"What about your dad?" I questioned gently.

"I loved him. And I know he'd be proud that his company is thriving. But I just can't grieve anymore. Even my mom has moved on. And she lost a son and a husband she loved. I need to enjoy the time I spend with her. She wants me to be happy."

Eli's mother was an incredible person, and I knew what he was saying was true.

"But there's a problem," he said.

"What?"

"I can't be happy without you, Butterfly."

My heart tripped as I asked, "What exactly does that mean?"

He took my hands and met my gaze. "It means how in the hell could you not know that I love you, too? I think I probably have for a long time, but I was too damn stupid to recognize it right away. The things I said in the beginning weren't me, Butterfly. I was still a shell of a man who was trying to cope with losing his twin brother and his father so close together. But it's no excuse. If you give me the opportunity, I'll make it up to you for the rest of our lives." He reached out and snatched the box from the coffee table where I'd dropped it to pick up my ice cream. "Which brings me to this."

He held out the box, and I took it with shaky fingers. I popped the lid and found myself staring at the most gorgeous diamond I'd ever seen. "Oh, my God. Eli? What is this?"

"You know what it is," he rasped. "Just put me out of my misery. Is it going to be a *yes* or a *no*?"

My heart was soaring as I threw myself into his arms. "Yes. Yes. God, I love you so much."

Eli's arms tightened around me immediately. "I love you, too, Butterfly. You fucking broke my heart today when you ran out of the office."

"Why didn't you say something sooner?"

He picked me up and flopped onto the couch with me. Eli held me like he was never going to let me go, and it made me cry even harder.

"I tried to tell you that I hadn't called you because I'd been too ill to talk, and those texts had been the mindless ramblings of a man who was trying to tell you how much you meant to me, but I failed because I couldn't form any coherent thoughts while I had a high fever. You didn't seem to want me to talk about anything personal. At that point, I was already terrified that I'd lost you. I was willing to settle for having you as my intern for a while if it meant I'd get to see you every day."

The text message really had been a mistake.

I threaded my hand into his hair because I had to touch him. "I was there because I wanted to be. You must have known I came to be an intern because of you."

"I wasn't quite sure what your motives were," he admitted. "But I was so damn happy to see you that I didn't want to scare you away. And then I ended up doing it anyway."

"I couldn't quite let you go, even after your text messages," I admitted. "I had to make sure that we were never going to work, and that you really wanted me to go."

He squeezed tightly. "I never wanted you to go anywhere. I always wanted you to stay, Jade. I guess I just didn't know how to change things. I think I was fucked from the first time you walked into my office and told me off."

"I thought you just wanted to fuck me," I teased.

"Oh, I did," he rumbled. "Still do. But I was a fool to think that I could just fuck you out of my system. There's never going to be a day when my dick doesn't get hard the second you walk into a room."

"You say the sweetest things," I said with a laugh.

"I'm not exactly good at saying sweet things," he answered with a frown.

I thought about all the nice things he'd done for me in the past, and the fact that he'd outright deeded the land that he couldn't previously let go of to me.

His actions said everything. "I was joking, Eli. The things you do matter."

"Then tell me what the hell to do to make you happy, because it's become a goddamn obsession for me."

"You already did it," I said. "But if you really want to make me happy, then take me to bed."

CHAPTER 29

JADE

Eli didn't waste any time. He got up and pulled me up with him.

"The ring first," he insisted as he took the box from my hand. "I need to know that you're going to be mine."

He pulled the ring out and dropped the box on the coffee table.

I started to sob as he put the gorgeous ring on my finger.

"Don't cry, Butterfly," he said huskily as he picked me up and carried me into my bedroom. "If I had my way, you'd never fucking cry again."

"I'm happy," I said. "They're happy tears this time."

"I can think of a lot better things we can do to be happy," he growled as he lowered me to my feet beside the bed.

"Then show me," I requested.

My body was already on fire, and he'd barely touched me. I was still having a hard time believing that Eli was really going to be mine.

He reached for the bottom of his sweater and pulled it over his head. "You own me, Jade. You know that, right?" he asked in a deep, sincere tone of voice.

I shuddered as I grabbed the sweater and tossed it on the floor. Eli was intentionally letting himself be vulnerable to me, and I'd never, ever betray that kind of trust.

I pulled the sweatshirt over my head and tossed that away, too, leaving me bare from the waist up.

"You own me, too, Eli," I told him.

Because the emotion between us was so intense, there was some kind of crazy primal need we both had to belong to each other. I could feel it thick in the air around us.

All I really wanted to do was surrender to it.

I wasn't afraid to give myself to Eli, any more than he minded letting me make him mine.

He snaked an arm around my waist and tugged me in until our upper bodies met skin-to-skin.

And it was bliss.

"You were always meant to be mine," he rasped before his head came down to capture my mouth.

I opened for him, and I wrapped my arms around his neck. I was greedy for the taste of him, every single bit of longing I'd harbored for weeks pouring from my lips to his.

I touched every inch of bare skin I could find, and then searched for more, my fingers exploring, trying desperately to bring Eli as close to me as I could possibly get him.

"Fuck!" he cursed when he'd lifted his hungry mouth from mine. "I need you, Jade."

I needed him, too, and he didn't resist when my fingers fumbled with the buttons of his jeans. They were tight because he was enormous and totally erect, but I managed to finally get them undone.

I dropped to my knees and practically clawed at the material to get it down his muscular legs, taking his boxer briefs with the jeans.

He kicked them aside as I palmed his enormous cock. I shivered as my fingers moved over what felt like silk over steel, and I bent forward to let my tongue taste the tiny bead of moisture on the tip.

I didn't get another taste because Eli hauled me to my feet.

The expression on his face was fierce as he said, "You have no idea how much I'd love to have those beautiful lips wrapped around me right now, but there's other things I want more."

"Like what?" I asked breathlessly.

"You," he grunted.

He reached for my shorts and tugged them down my legs until they were bunched at my ankles so I could kick them off.

His eyes roamed over me possessively as he said, "I've never seen anything as beautiful as you."

I shivered as his hands cupped my breasts, his thumbs tracing over my hard nipples. He squeezed them for a moment and then let go, and the painful pleasure made my core clench with a need so savage that it was overwhelming.

His hand slipped between my thighs, and he was met by nothing but wet heat.

"God, baby, you're so damn wet."

I closed my eyes and moaned, helpless, as his finger slid over my clit. "Eli," I whimpered, my longing for him so deep that it was almost scary.

His fingers were merciless, every stroke driving me higher and higher.

I let out a whine when he suddenly stopped, lifted me, and tumbled us both onto the bed.

In an instant, his mouth was where his finger had been, and it was scorching hot as he buried his head between my legs.

There was no gentle teasing. He devoured me with a white-hot passion that made me half-crazy.

Eli wasn't tentative in anything he did, but when he threw himself into my pleasure, it felt so good it was almost unbearable.

His tongue moved in a carnal, ravenous motion, over and over on the tiny bundle of nerves that was screaming for attention.

My climax rushed up to meet me so quickly that I was mewling nonsense as my thighs began to shake.

His fingers slid inside me, and he curled them until he hit a spot that sent me careening over the edge.

"Oh-my-God-I'm-not-going-to-live-through-this," I screamed.

My back and hips arched off the bed as my orgasm steamrolled over me.

I was a panting mess after my climax had chewed me up and spit me out.

But it had only made me all the more desperate to get Eli inside me.

"Okay?" Eli asked gruffly as he moved up my body.

"Fuck me, Eli," I pleaded.

I was feeling desperate.

He pulled me on top of him. "Ride me, baby," he demanded.

I straddled him eagerly, but I had no experience with the position. "I don't know what to do," I confessed.

He grasped my hips and lowered me down until I could feel the tip of his cock against my sex.

I lowered myself down, savoring every single inch until he was buried to his balls.

"Yes," I hissed as I balanced myself with my hands on his shoulders.

It felt like he was buried so deep that he'd never come out. But he proved me wrong as he guided my hips to pull out, and then sink down on him again.

We moved just like that together, Eli pushing up as I sank down, every thrust slow and deep.

I purred, my carnal urges momentarily satisfied, but I still wanted more.

My eyes roamed over Eli's face, relishing the intense pleasure I saw there. I straightened up and leaned back as he increased the pace, noticing that he had his legs bent so I could rest against them for support.

I closed my eyes and tilted my head back, getting lost in the erotic pleasure of the steadily increasing rhythm that was threatening to tear me apart.

"Fuck, Jade," Eli growled. "It's too damn good."

I leaned forward again, putting my hands on his chest. "Just come, Eli," I said. "Don't hold back."

"I'll never come without you," he said roughly as he reached a hand between our bodies and found my clit.

It took very little stimulation to set me off.

My channel clenched hard around Eli's cock as I shuddered my way to climax.

He tightened his hold on my hips and started to slam his hips up in a frenzied pace while he put a hand around the back of my neck and pulled my mouth down for a kiss that tasted like love, lust, hot and sweaty sex, and intense orgasm.

I lay sprawled across his chest, my body totally spent as I tried to catch my breath.

My entire body was limp, but Eli was cradling me protectively, so I knew I'd eventually recover.

When I could move, I slid to Eli's side, and his arm tightened around me again.

Emotions welled up inside me, and they were all so jumbled that I couldn't identify much except the love that I had for the man who had just completely rocked my world.

"I love you," I told him.

"I love you, too, baby," he answered.

It was the last thing I remembered hearing before I fell asleep.

CHAPTER 30

Jade

"How is it that I never heard about Austin?" I asked carefully as Eli and I ate breakfast the next morning. "I never even knew you had a twin at all, much less that he was addicted to drugs."

I watched as Eli devoured the eggs, bacon, and pancakes I'd just put in front of him moments before.

He was easy to stare at since he'd only pulled on a pair of jeans and was shirtless.

He paused and downed some of his coffee before he spoke. "My parents tried to protect both Austin and me from the media. My dad worked especially hard on keeping my brother's addiction problem a family issue. They kept a low profile and pretty much just worked. The press had nothing to talk about."

"Until you broke out with crazy stuff," I said.

He nodded. "I *wanted* the attention because of my charities, and I managed to attract a lot of celebrities and athletes for my events. Especially racing. The events got a lot of publicity."

I sat down, and we were quiet for a few minutes as we ate. When I finally put my fork down, I said, "I'm full."

I had to wonder whether I still had Ben & Jerry's overload from the night before.

He lifted an eyebrow. "What happened to my woman who likes to eat?"

"I ate plenty," I answered, and then swiped his empty plate and pushed mine in front of him. "Can you finish it?"

"After last night, I'm pretty sure I can," he teased.

"You need to keep up your energy," I agreed, watching as he plowed through the rest of my uneaten food.

"Do you have any complaints?" he rumbled.

I sighed. "Not one."

Eli could surpass any of the romance heroes I read about. In fact, he was so much more than I'd ever imagined. He was relentless, and we'd both been greedy all night long. I doubted that I could ever get enough of him, even though every part of my body was sore from overuse. And I was exhausted because we only slept for short periods throughout the night.

"Unless you want me to burn all this energy I just put in, I suggest you wear something other than my sweater."

The garment was so warm, and I never wanted to take it off because it smelled like Eli.

"I'll get it cleaned," I told him with a smile.

"Baby, I'm not worried about clean clothes. I have stuff next door. But every time you bend over, I can see that gorgeous ass."

"Is that a problem for you?" I provoked.

He gave me a deliciously dangerous look. "You know it is," he said in a raspy voice.

There was something incredibly wicked about poking the beast, and Eli could become an alpha caveman in a New York minute.

To be honest, I loved bringing out the impatient, dominant male side of him. It wasn't the least bit daunting, because he only became that man with me. And it was the hottest damn thing I'd ever seen.

I got up and started clearing the table, and I could feel his eyes watching me as I repeatedly and purposely bent over to reach across the space.

When I was done, I moved next to him and bent to pick up an imaginary piece of lint on the floor.

He was on me before I could blink.

I savored the feel of his powerful chest pressing against my back, and his jean-clad erection against my rear.

"You were warned, Butterfly," he growled into my ear.

"I guess I wasn't all that scared," I said breathlessly as I placed my hands flat on the table.

I trembled as his hand stroked over my ass.

"I still don't know whether to spank this or fucking worship it," he rasped, his voice heavy with need.

"Maybe both," I suggested hopefully.

Eli turned me on no matter how he touched me, and I didn't suppose it would be any different if he slapped my ass. As long as he fucked me after he was done.

He pressed gently on my back, lowering my upper body to the wood surface and making my ass go up in the air.

I don't think I was quite ready for the feel of his big, strong hand connecting with my ass.

I yelped as it connected, even though the pain was minimal.

The sharp tingle of his hand slapping my vulnerable butt cheeks was so erotic that I moaned.

It was in no way a punishment. He smacked it a couple more times, caressing the globes sensually every time he met my flesh.

When he reached between my thighs, I was almost disappointed, but the lingering sting ramped up the pleasure of him stroking my saturated folds and zeroing in on arousing me by rubbing hard against my clit.

"Eli," I moaned. "Fuck me," I demanded.

I could feel him fumbling with his jeans as he rumbled, "I'll never fucking get tired of hearing you say that."

Maybe I shouldn't have been, but I was shocked as he drove himself home from behind.

The angle was so incredibly different, and he was so deep that I gasped.

"Yes," I encouraged.

My tight channel accepted him, and there were no preliminaries. Both of us were too hungry, too needy.

I pushed back against him, finding my own rhythm as he impaled me over and over again.

"Harder," I begged.

"I don't want to hurt you," he growled.

"You won't. I need you, Eli."

Incredibly, he grasped my hips even more forcefully and hammered into me at a pace that had me rising toward climax.

When he reached a hand around my body and caressed my clit, I imploded.

"I love you so damn much, Jade," he grunted.

Those words flowed over my shaking body and invaded my soul.

"I love you, too," I said on a sharply drawn breath as my core spasmed so hard I could barely breathe.

He roared incoherently as I milked him to his own powerful orgasm.

Eli stayed buried deep inside of me for a moment, and then scooped my limp body up and sank into one of the dining-room chairs.

"I'm fucking hopeless," he said in a graveled voice. "I could never survive without you anymore, sweetheart."

He held me like I was his most precious treasure, and I could feel the emotion emanating from his body.

"You don't have to," I said in a voice husky with postorgasmic satisfaction. "I'll always be here."

He kissed me softly, lingering over my lips tenderly.

"Damn good thing," he answered. "But you really have to stop bending over stuff. You'll give me a heart attack."

I smiled against his shoulder. There was something sinfully appealing about the fact that I could bring a powerful man like Eli to his knees. And he trusted me enough to let me know it.

"God, I'm sore," I shared as I stood up slowly and stretched.

He frowned. "Why didn't you say something?"

"I didn't want to stop."

He stood. "Hot tub. Now."

"I don't have a hot tub," I informed him.

"Then it's a good thing I own the house next door that does have one," he said with a grin.

I smiled back at him, utterly happy that Eli had made that purchase that I'd once found to be crazy extravagant.

Maybe it hadn't been such a bad idea after all.

CHAPTER 31

AIDEN

I tried to stand through the tuxedo fitting patiently, but I wasn't the type of guy who had an easy time standing still.

I can do this for Jade.

My baby sister was getting married at the end of the summer.

Brooke had been first.

And now Jade was tying the knot with the man Seth and I had just partnered with to amass what we hoped would eventually be the biggest building-and-real-estate business in the world.

Truth be told, I liked Eli Stone and so did Seth. But I wasn't crazy about being part of the wedding party.

Best man.

I'd gotten the supposed honor of standing up for Eli since most of his close friends were out of state. The majority of them were planning on attending, but couldn't be around for all of the other festivities.

"Ouch!" I said grumpily as another errant pin stuck me in the ass.

"Sorry, Mr. Sinclair. Almost done," the female who was altering the monkey suit said in a remorseful voice.

"Not a big deal," I grumbled, feeling bad that I'd bit her head off.

But I wasn't exactly in a serene mood.

My gaze was drawn to the other side of the room for about the hundredth time since I'd arrived at the tailor's.

As usual, my eyes locked onto the hottest blonde I'd ever seen. Actually, I'd done far more to the woman's body years ago than ogle it. I'd once been deep inside her virginal form, and my dick wasn't ever going to let me forget it.

Skye Weston, Jade's bridesmaid, had once been the only woman I wanted.

Now, she was the only female I wanted to forget.

"All done, sir," the seamstress said. "If you can take it off carefully, I can get it altered."

"Yeah. Got it," I told her as I strode back into a dressing room, and then breathed a sigh of relief once I was back into a pair of jeans and a sweater.

I'd spent my entire adult life working as a longline commercial fisherman, sometimes working fourteen to eighteen hours a day for trips that could last over two months.

I wasn't exactly into tuxedos and cocktail parties, even though I was, through some damn miracle I still didn't completely accept, a billionaire.

Somehow I knew I'd probably always be a fisherman at heart. Maybe I'd clean up well, but I'd never quite be as casual in a tux as somebody like Eli Stone.

I exited the dressing room just in time to see Skye coming out of hers in a pair of jeans and a green sweater that I already knew matched her eyes.

Get over it, Sinclair.

My relationship with her happened a long time ago. It had been almost a decade. But for some reason, she was the only woman I wished had stayed.

Maybe I was still pissed that she left me while I was out on a long-haul trip. If I wanted to be reasonable, it wasn't easy dating a guy like me. I had been at sea more than I was home, and I'd made shit for money. But the funds I'd taken in had helped raise my siblings, so I couldn't ever regret doing it.

Just talk to her so you can both be civil for Jade's wedding.

Not a single word had passed between me and Skye since she'd moved back to Citrus Beach from San Diego. Strangely, she'd appeared to be just as angry as I was, and had dissed me every time we ran into each other.

I stopped next to her instead of going for the door. "Hello, Skye," I greeted her cautiously.

Her face looked tense as she stared at me. "Aiden," she acknowledged.

"Look, I know that we have an unpleasant past, but can we just get along until Jade's wedding is over?" I asked huskily. "Our relationship was over a long time ago, and we've both moved on."

Christ! I'm such a liar.

Honestly, I really wanted to take her and shake her until she told me why the hell she'd married another guy, a man who had evidently put her and her daughter through hell. Shit! I would have been a better choice, even though I'd been poor. At least I wasn't part of an organized-crime ring. And I'd cared about her.

She turned her head, her eyes darting away from mine. "I'm not over it, and you know why," she said in a sharp tone I'd never heard her utter. "But I have no problem trying to be civil for Jade's sake. Now I have to go. I have a daughter to pick up from school."

"What in the hell did I do?" I asked in an angry voice. "You left me, remember?"

"Obviously you have a memory problem," she answered as she put on her lightweight jacket. "I'll see you at the wedding."

I gaped at her as her shapely ass marched out the door.

"What the fuck?" I said under my breath.

She has no damn reason to hate me. I didn't replace her with another woman. She dumped me while I was out to sea.

If there was one thing I knew, it was that Skye was a realist. And she wasn't prone to drama. At least, she hadn't been.

Something's not right.

I strode to the door and exited just in time to see the back of her car as she drove away.

Why the fuck do I care?

Skye Weston was nothing to me anymore.

I put my hands in the pockets of my jeans, determined that I wasn't going to give a shit about why she seemed to blame me for our breakup.

But as I headed for my vehicle, I knew damn well I was lying to myself.

Skye had haunted me for years, so I was going to figure out exactly what she was thinking. I just wasn't entirely sure how I was going to do it.

EPILOGUE

JADE

Three months later . . .

"Eli, are you seriously considering this project?" I asked him as I went through a prospectus on a large research facility that was less than five years old and failing.

I hadn't yet snagged the job of my dreams, even though I'd interviewed for several over the last few months. Some of them had been out of the area, a move that Eli wasn't particularly happy about. But he was so supportive that he offered to have dual headquarters if I was interested in any of the opportunities.

Honestly, I didn't want to go anywhere. San Diego and Citrus Beach were home for both of us. And even though I knew he'd do anything for me, I knew he didn't want to live on the opposite coast, and neither did I.

I was still getting used to the fact that I was marrying Eli. We spent the weekdays in his San Diego home, and the weekends in Citrus Beach. I was still helping him out in his office every day because he insisted that he needed me, but I knew it was just an excuse for both of us to work together every day.

I was getting better and better at handling some things at Stone, but I was mostly still vetting the opportunities that came up on a daily basis.

"I really don't know," he said nonchalantly from his desk. "I thought I'd leave that one up to you. It's not in my area of expertise."

I looked up from my position on the couch across the room. "You have experts," I reminded him.

"I'd rather have you take it," he answered.

I went back to my laptop and finished going through the information I had. Finally, I said, "It looks like they took on way too many projects, and didn't have the money to fund them."

It was a state-of-the-art genetics lab, but it was poorly managed.

"If I decided to buy, I think it would make an excellent facility to do genetic conservation research for wildlife," he said.

It took me a moment to take in what Eli was really suggesting.

The facility was enormous, and could accommodate several areas of study. Since it was already built, there would be minimal changes needed, but overall it was perfect.

"The facility is amazing, but do you realize what it costs to keep a nonprofit like this going?" I asked. "It would take an enormous amount of continual fund-raising."

He turned his head and grinned at me. "I kind of know a guy who's pretty good at that. And I have some donors already lined up. Most of them are Sinclairs, but it wouldn't be hard to find more."

My mind started to spin as I thought about all the good that could be done with this facility. "I need connections worldwide for sample swaps and field research."

"I'll get you the numbers," he said confidently. "And you'll build those relationships, sweetheart. It doesn't happen overnight."

My eyes welled up with tears as I thought about getting back into the lab to find solutions for dwindling populations of wildlife. I'd need to build a strong team around me. But it could be done.

Never in my life had I believed I could do something that could have so much impact on conservation. And being offered the opportunity to do that made my heart feel like it was being tightened in a vise.

"So you already called in the troops to donate?" I asked softly.

"Didn't have to," he replied. "Your brothers and Brooke were on board immediately, and then the rest of the family got in line to sign up for it. They all know how passionate you are about conservation, and they all truly believe you'll be doing important work. It's a cause everybody can get behind, sweetheart. The only one who can stop it is you."

I'd gotten in my own way many times in my life, but I wasn't about to do it now. "I want it. I really do want it," I said as I rose to my feet with tears trickling down my face.

I raced across the room, and Eli was already standing with his arms wide open.

He caught me, just like I knew he would.

"I love you," I said happily and I wrapped my arms around him and squeezed him as hard as I could. "How did I ever get lucky enough to be marrying somebody like you?"

"I was thinking the same thing, but for the life of me, I can't figure it out," he teased. "For some reason, you think I'm somebody special, and I'm not about to clue you in on the truth."

I laughed as I punched his arm playfully. Eli had made my causes his, too, and he'd always kept my spirits up when I couldn't find the job I wanted.

"You basically built this job for me," I accused.

"No, I didn't. You're fucking brilliant, Jade. And if anybody can save some animals that are headed for extinction, it's you. You honestly need your own facility, and it doesn't hurt that you have a huge family of billionaires. That opportunity was there for you all along. I just wasn't sure it was what you wanted."

"It never really occurred to me, Eli. I'm not a big-picture thinker."

"Only because you've never had the opportunity to think big," he said huskily. "Now you do. I propose that you name it the Sinclair Institute for Wildlife Conservation."

"The Sinclair-Stone Institute," I corrected. "I'm not going to be a Sinclair much longer. And you made this all happen, Eli. Thank you."

What else could I say to the man who had already given me the world, and then offered me even more? There weren't really words to describe how much he meant to me, not because he was rich, but because he was Eli.

"I didn't really do that much. I found the opportunity, and I'm buying the facility. But there wouldn't be a research center if you weren't the most intelligent and driven person I know."

"I'm going to be busy," I warned him.

"I have to negotiate and purchase the company first," he said. "And I don't care if you're busy, as long as you always come home to me."

"I can do some things once we own the rights, and then build a team and decide on projects once we get back from our honeymoon."

Eli was taking me to Australia, another one of my dream destinations. A place I wasn't even sure I'd ever visit because I thought I'd be paying off student loans for decades.

"What did you decide about the DNA match?" he asked. "Are you going to tell your family?"

I'd never heard back from whoever had matched my DNA. And months had passed now. If I told my siblings, I knew they wouldn't have any idea which one of them was responsible. "I'm not sure it would do any good. My brothers obviously don't know, or they would have been with their child. I don't know if it's better or not to burden them if we don't know who it is."

"I'm willing to do some digging," he offered. "I can probably get to somebody who can give me some information."

The fact that I had a niece somewhere in the world had been bothering me, and Eli knew it. "Yes, please," I answered. "I'd like to know her if I can find out where she is. And my brothers are in the position to help now. If I can get anything about her, I could probably figure out which brother is the father."

"Now that Aiden, Seth, and I are starting up the new corporation, I spend a lot of time with both of them. Maybe I can get something out of them without spilling the beans."

I rolled my eyes. "Good luck with that. All of my brothers are pretty closemouthed about their love lives, even if they don't have a problem jumping into mine."

"They'll have no choice but to back out of it now," he said drily. "I'll be damned if they're going to stand guard over you. That's my job now."

"It's nobody's job," I retorted. "I'm perfectly capable of taking care of myself. And speaking of that, what can I do to take care of you, Mr. Stone? Since you've just made my dreams come true, I really want to do something for you."

"You know the only thing I ever want is to get you naked," he said huskily.

I smiled at him and tightened my arms around his neck. That was *not* the only thing Eli wanted, but he did think about it an awful lot. Maybe as much as I did.

"I want to make *you* happy," I told him.

"Way too late for that, Butterfly. I'm already happier than I could have ever imagined."

He'd changed so much in the last few months, and he seemed much more content with who he was now. Eli talked openly and often about Austin, and there were pictures of his brother everywhere in his home.

Although he still did some dangerous things, they weren't as outrageous as his previous pursuits. I was learning to rock climb along with him, but I drew the line at auto racing. I had bitten my fingernails to the quick when he'd done a celebrity racing event for charity last month, but I'd gotten through it.

The guy had a thing for fast cars, but I could live with that.

I was just glad he'd cancelled the challenge to swim the English Channel and the insanely dangerous multiskill race across the wilds of Patagonia.

Eli kept the crazy going for charity, but he was doing only the things he personally enjoyed.

"I love you," I said, the declaration coming from the depths of my soul.

He nodded. "I know. That's why I'm so damn happy. Because I love you, too, Butterfly."

I kind of feel like a butterfly.

He lowered his head and kissed me, and I spread my wings a little further.

I'd come a long way from the woman I'd been just months ago, and it had nothing to do with my inheritance.

Eli had slowly pried me out of my shy, unconfident cocoon of confusion. Maybe I'd taken a few missteps along the way, but the night I'd agreed to let Eli show me his world had sealed my fate.

Even then, when he was a noncommitment kind of guy, I'd still instinctively trusted him.

I threaded my hands through his hair and kissed him back.

As long as I had this man who loved me so fiercely, I knew I was always going to keep flying higher.

We'd always be soaring side by side.

ACKNOWLEDGMENTS

Once again, my thanks to my incredible team at Montlake Romance. This entire journey has been amazing, and I'm so grateful to be sharing it with the Montlake team, who make every one of my books as good as it can be.

A huge shout-out to my extraordinary editor, Maria Gomez. Thank you for everything you do for me and for my books.

As usual, I'm incredibly grateful for my KA team and my street team, Jan's Gems. I'm not sure how to express my thanks to all of you, so I'll just go with my usual . . . you rock!

XXXXX Jan

ABOUT THE AUTHOR

Photo © 2013 by Carrie Herzog

J.S. "Jan" Scott is the *New York Times* and *USA Today* bestselling author of numerous contemporary and paranormal romances, including The Sinclairs series. She's an avid reader of all types of books and literature, but romance has always been her genre of choice—so she writes what she loves to read: stories that are almost always steamy, generally feature an alpha male, and have a happily ever after, because she just can't seem to write them any other way! Jan loves to connect with readers. Visit her website at www.authorjsscott.com.